A
Clown
Like Me

Also by Joan L. Oppenheimer
Gardine vs. Hanover

by Joan L. Oppenheimer

A
Clown
Like Me

THOMAS Y. CROWELL   New York

Library of Congress Cataloging in Publication Data
Oppenheimer, Joan L.
  A clown like me.

  Summary: Upon donning their individual clown personas
in a 4-H clowning class, three teen-aged girls
unexpectedly discover interpersonal strengths that they
never dreamed existed.
  [1. Clowns—Fiction. 2. Friendship—Fiction.
3. Self-perception—Fiction] I. Title.
PZ7.622Cl 1985   [Fic]   82-45577
ISBN 0-690-04283-3
ISBN 0-690-04284-1 (lib. bdg.)

*To Lisa and Nancy Main
and all of the other 4-H clowns*

1

If they ever run my life history through a computer, the printout will begin with three vital facts: (*1*) I was born on April 1, (*2*) I've always been in the middle, and (*3*) I'm medium/average/ordinary in every way.

I figure anybody born on April Fool's Day is practically fated to be a clown. Something like that marks you from the beginning, unless you're blessed with a lot more strength of character than I have.

It would not be accurate to say that I finally buckled under pressure, or had strong signals from the moon and planets and stars—all that good astrology stuff. There was nothing gradual about it. I've been a clown as long as I can remember.

That's partly because I'm a middle child, two years younger than my brother Byron, who's seventeen and mean as a snake, and four years older than my sister Emily, who has a fat brain and a big mouth. There are three of us, Byron and Emily and me, Shelley. The names probably give you the impression that my mother is (*1*) hung up on poets and (*2*) sort of a squirrel. You'd be right on both counts.

She's also a fantastic mother. Don't get the idea that I'm a rotten kid who hates her own family. Both my parents are neat. Even Byron and Emily have their moments. To be totally honest, however, I have to add that in the last couple years those moments are so rare, they're etched in gold in my memory.

Mom just laughs and says we're all still going through phases. Maybe so, but if you ask me, both Byron and Emily would make the *Guinness Book of World Records* if they had a category for Longest Running Phases Known for Kids 11–17. Anyway, you can see I had to have a sense of humor, merely to survive in a central position with a home environment that waxes to wild and wanes to weird.

I'm also in the middle between my two best friends, Nicole and Megan. Nicole is older, almost sixteen, taller, and stunningly beautiful. Megan is younger, still fourteen, shorter, and a mouse. Homely, too. Nicole and I would punch out anybody else who said that, but privately we have to admit it's true.

Where does that leave me? Remember what I said about being average and medium and ordinary? That's the bottom line on Shelley Elizabeth Lucas. (Did you catch the middle name? That's for Elizabeth Barrett Browning. My mother didn't miss a trick.)

If you want the gruesome statistics: I have hair that's a nothing shade between almost brown and a little bit blond, sometimes reddish in bright sunlight; eyes that are blue or gray or green, depending on the color I wear; average height, medium weight, ordinary intelligence. Wishy-washy, colorless, dull. As far as looks are concerned, I'd get lost in a crowd of two.

There's only one thing to do when you realize fate has dealt a lousy hand like that. You develop a bizarre personality, the anything-for-a-laugh trip. At least I did.

Even my kindergarten teacher used to break up laughing at me. In fact, she's the first person who used the magic word in my hearing. She told my mother one day, "Shelley's sure a refreshing change from my shy kids or the ones who cry every day for a week. Shelley's a *clown!*"

With my track record as a Funny Girl who worked

hard for the name and reputation, you'd expect me to be first in line to sign up for a class in Clownology. Wrong. When Nicole and Megan first mentioned the 4-H class in clowning, I thought it was a terrible idea.

In Mesa Vista, a town midway between Los Angeles and San Diego, most of the kids are into 4-H projects. We'd already had cooking and cake decorating and sewing. Megan loves animals, so she's raised everything from guinea pigs to rabbits to lambs. This class would be something unique. Nicole and Megan were excited about it from the moment they heard Mrs. De Witt had agreed to be the leader.

They talked me into it about three weeks before school started. Megan and I had gone over to swim in the pool at Nicole's condo. We almost always had it to ourselves in the afternoon. The little kids were in taking naps, and the only people outside were either old ladies sitting in the whirlpool or younger ones flaked out on lounges on the adjoining lawn.

The three of us made so much noise playing water tag that Tilly Tyler came out on the balcony to flap her arms and tell us to be quiet, Granny Gus was resting. Nicole lives with her grandmother. Her name is Augusta, so everyone calls her Granny Gus. Tilly is Granny's housekeeper-companion, also a kind of distant cousin. They're both really nice.

4

We realized we'd been whooping it up pretty good, so we got out of the water and lay on our towels, heads together in our usual Y formation.

"You better quit dragging your feet about the clown class, Shell." Nicole sat up to squeeze water out of her long braid. "Mrs. De Witt has fifteen kids signed up, and she can't take more than twenty."

I groaned. "You guys are serious about this class? What's so great about putting a lot of glop on your face and dressing up silly to make people laugh? Right now, I go to all kinds of trouble to look *terrific*, and still everybody cracks up the minute they see me."

"No, they only do that when you say something crazy," Megan said quietly. "You're actually a very pretty girl."

She's the peacemaker on the rare occasions when Nicole and I square off for a brief skirmish. Megan's also our private, personal cheerleader. Sometimes I do a number on my flaws on purpose, just because it's so consoling to hear Megan argue with me.

"There's only one area on my whole entire bod that's pretty," I said. "Totally perfect, in fact."

Nicole grinned and Megan rolled her eyes, but neither of them would play straight man for me.

"I'll tell you, anyway," I said, miffed. "It's a little strip of skin about a quarter inch square between my eighth and ninth vertebrae. Unfortunately, very few people ever see it except for you clods. And you don't appreciate—"

"Shell." Nicole stared at me. Even slightly blood-shot from chlorine, her wide-spaced blue eyes were lovely, thick dark lashes damp and tangled from her swim. "Shell, you're a natural for this class. What is there about it that turns you off?" She handed Megan the tube of sunscreen and turned her flaw-less back and shoulders so Megan could apply it.

"Does a bus driver ride the bus on his day off?" I made a face. "Why should I be all that thrilled about a class in clowning?"

"It's not the same thing you do," Megan said. "Not at all. You're a person who's naturally funny. This is—it's just a kind of exaggeration. Anybody can learn clowning, I guess, but some people are going to be better at it than others. And you'd be sensational." She turned her back and sat cross-legged so Nicole could put sunscreen on her, too.

"Besides," Nicole said, "it wouldn't be as much fun without all three of us. Whatever happened to your club spirit?" She caught my puzzled glance. "First Friends Forever," she said solemnly. But her eyes were full of laughter.

"Oh, wow. Now you're bringing up the heavy artillery. Talk about a guilt trip. Nine on the scale." But I had to laugh. I hadn't thought about that nutty third-grade club of ours for ages.

First Friends Forever we called it, and it was an absurdly exclusive group. Nobody could join unless they had a birthday on the first of the month. That was our way of limiting membership to Megan (October 1), Nicole (December 1), and me, because of my April Fool's Day debut.

We fought for each other, boosted each other, adored each other. That didn't change even after the little club faded into memory. Nicole had reminded me, however, of the solemn vow we'd made to BE THERE FOR EACH OTHER. First Friends Forever.

"This class is for junior high kids, too," I said darkly, "and fifth- and sixth-graders. That means Emily, the Motor Mouth. She's been dying to join something that I'm in. And I will be so *humiliated*—" My voice went up to a squeak. "That kid talks so much, her lips need a retread every six months."

"You think Miz De Witt can't handle your sister Emily?" Megan laughed. "Listen, if our fearless leader ever debated Gloria Steinem or—or even Bella Abzug, you'd have to feel sorry for poor Gloria and Bella. She'd take them apart at the seams."

I grinned at that interesting picture. Mrs. De Witt is little and blond and cute. And a marvelous 4-H leader. She gets a project moving, keeps it on track, and helps solve all the problems. But she's not only a dynamo, she's big on discipline. Right from the first day, she's in charge, and heaven help anybody

7

who tries to take over. Godzilla would back off from that lady, babbling apologies every step of the way.

"It might be worth it," I said, "just to see how she muzzles Emily."

"Then you'll do it? You'll call Mrs. De Witt the minute you get home?" Megan saw me nod and sat back with a small satisfied smile.

"Promise?" Nicole had to pin it down. She's a lot more insecure than Megan is.

Actually, we all were insecure, but about different things. Megan knew very well she was a mouse, and a little plain gray one at that. I battled the clown complex, though I didn't know why. Nicole was wary of people. She couldn't truly trust anybody but Granny and Tilly and Megan and me. I suppose she wondered if it would ever be any different. The way I figure, that must be the scariest kind of insecurity.

"I promise," I said wearily. "I swear. I'll write it in blood if you find the donor. I don't feel up to opening a vein at the moment."

Two hours later, I called Mrs. De Witt. Shamed into it, you might say, because neither Megan nor Nicole made any further attempts to reinforce my promise. I can't stand it when people blindly trust me and all the while I'm trying to think of some way to weasel out of a commitment.

Mrs. De Witt put my name down and told me I

was Number Twenty. Nobody else could join the class. That cheered me enormously. I figured that took care of the Littlest Lucas.

Then Mrs. De Witt said, "You must be Emily's sister. She called this morning while I was out. My daughter put her name on the list."

"Wonderful," I said in my brightest voice. "Emily will be so pleased."

She was, of course. At the dinner table, she went on and on about the history of clowns. Naturally she'd been at the library all day, boning up. When she isn't talking, my sister has her nose in a book, gathering material for her next monologue. Emily should consider donating her brain for medical research when she shoves off to the next world. I bet they'd find more cellulite than gray cells.

"People always like to have clowns around," she babbled that night, "even though they weren't always called clowns."

"Yes, they go back as far as we've recorded history," my mother said, "maybe even further. We know they were in ancient Rome with the theater and circuses. After that, there were traveling performers who sang and told stories. Jugglers and tumblers went around the countryside. And of course there's the tradition of fools and jesters in the courts of kings and queens."

"Right," Emily said, looking startled. It always

9

seems to surprise her when she realizes someone else knows as much as she does. "Kings and queens used to *collect* people who were really good at poetry and music, singing or playing some instrument. They'd trade them like—like a really good horse or dog. Or give them away as gifts. I think that's gross."

I drifted off when she went into detail about dwarfs and grotesques, people who were physically deformed or mentally defective, kept around to amuse the court. It only proved that nothing much is new under the sun. We still have bigotry and a few bent brains, too, who seem to find something funny about handicapped or retarded people.

Sometimes I can turn down the sound when Emily's expounding at the dinner table, and it's possible to watch her without absorbing the zillions of words that pour out of her. She's already quite pretty at eleven and a lot more coordinated than I am. It's as if Mom got it all together the third time around. Knowing it would be her last baby, she gave it her best shot.

Emily's going to knock the socks off every guy around with her big shiny eyes. No shilly-shallying about their color. They aren't green or blue, but gray and huge and dramatic. Great hair, too. And perfect teeth without the hardware routine that Byron and I went through.

10

It can be pure pain, having a sister like that, especially one who corrects your pronunciation. You know how infuriating it is when somebody leaps in to supply the word you're groping for? Yeah, she does that, too.

She'll have to find out the hard way that she may get those gorgeous teeth rearranged someday if she doesn't stop spouting off about every last thing she knows. Guys may salivate a lot, just looking at her. But ten minutes into a one-sided discussion, and she'll find she's lost her audience.

At about this point, she paused for breath and to inhale some food, so Dad entered the conversation. He's big and easygoing, but rather stern looking. It always fractures people when they discover his goofy sense of humor.

"I did a paper once on Henry VIII," he said. "Every time his name is mentioned, you think about all the wives. Everybody knows about them. So I looked for another angle, and I found it in Henry's fool. William Somers. Ever hear about him?"

"Why, no," my mother said. "That sounds interesting. What year are we talking about?" She turned to my brother, silent as usual, his whole attention on eating. "Byron, can you guess?"

I sometimes wonder if Byron and I both were gifted with this tuning-out ability as a defense mechanism because fate knew what was in store for us:

11

Emily. Byron is only interested in sports and girls and food, in that order, so we have his physical presence among us but not much else.

"Ask him the year the Dodgers won the first pennant," Emily said. "Ask him the batting average for anybody who's played ball for the last ten years—" She saw my father giving her the evil eye and subsided.

My Dad has dark bristling brows and a formidable nose. He has a deformed vocal cord, so his voice can go from a normal tone directly to a bellow. It's a great way to drown out Emily but it hurts her feelings, so he gives her fair warning by way of The Look.

Byron said now, predictably, "What? Who? What're you talking about?"

"Henry VIII and his jester, William Somers," Dad said. "Ever hear of him?"

"No."

"Your mother wondered if you could guess what year he came to Henry's court."

"Oh." Byron finished his milk and leaned back, touching the scar over his left eyebrow. He totaled his first car and that scar's a memento. It fascinates all the girls. "I'd say 1500—maybe later—make it 1520."

Dad grinned. "Close. 1525."

Emily sniffed. "Lucky guess. You said you never

heard of William Somers. I bet you've been learning about Henry VIII in school, and you just happened to remember the date and—"

"You'll never know, will you?" Byron glowered at her, excused himself, and left the table. He didn't glower because she'd ticked him off. That just happens to be his habitual expression. He's a strawberry blond like Mom, but he got Dad's thick eyebrows and intense blue eyes. Also, Dad's nose.

Thank goodness, Emily and I lucked out with miniature versions. We have small faces, and we sure don't need a half pound of nose right in the center.

Dad went on to tell us more about Henry's fool. William Somers wasn't a dwarf, more of a hunchback, very small and thin and stooped. He became a national figure, and people wrote songs and plays about him. Henry seemed to like him better than anybody else. They went riding and made up verses together. When the king was older, he suffered from gout. Often he wouldn't let anybody near him but William.

As I listened, I decided the nicest thing about William Somers was the fact that he never wanted the limelight and never abused the privileges that came to him as the king's favorite. It must have been fun, living at court and having anything he wanted. Then I remembered that William Somers never had the freedom to leave. Most people wouldn't choose his kind of life, even with all the goodies.

It was my turn for kitchen duty, so I went out to load the dishwasher. Later, in my room, I could still hear Emily's voice droning over the sound of the news on TV.

Before I went to sleep that night, I wondered how Mrs. De Witt would keep my sister quiet during the clown class. Then I remembered what Nicole had asked when they were trying to talk me into joining the class. "What is there about it that turns you off?"

I wouldn't have the answer to that one for a long time.

2

By the following Tuesday, the three of us managed to collect all the paraphernalia we'd been told to bring to the first class. That included a three-ring notebook and a case large enough to carry everything we'd need to make up: cold cream, baby oil, the greasepaint we'd use (Clown White, Clown Black, and Clown Red), baby powder, eyebrow pencil, sponge, brush, and a makeup mirror. Mrs. De Witt said we could get all of it for under ten dollars if we shopped around.

She wanted mothers to attend that first class, too, if possible. My mom wouldn't go back to her job as school secretary for another week, so that worked out okay.

Mrs. Malloncrodt, Megan's mother, could come, too. She's very social, but she schedules her time so she's usually home whenever her kids are. The thing that irritates me is that she seems a lot more interested in Megan's little brothers than she is in Meg.

Riley and Tim are pesty, noisy, and grubby, and their sense of humor can only be described as crude. In other words, typical little boys. They're cute looking, though, and Megan's mother is pretty, too. I can't help but wonder if it bothers Mrs. Malloncrodt that Megan is a mouse.

Anyway, our two mothers told Granny Gus they'd stand in for Nicole's mom, who lives about thirty miles away in another condo above Fashion Valley, where she owns a very expensive dress shop. Talk about a weird arrangement.

It seems Mrs. Wesley divorced Nicole's father when Nico was five. Granny figured it might be pretty traumatic for her, so she whisked her away to Europe. (That's why she's nearly a year older than I am, and she didn't start school with us till second grade.) Thing is, her mother never did come to take her home. Nico continued to live with Granny and Tilly. I figure she's lucky. Her mom is gorgeous, but so cold she'd freeze your eyelashes at twenty paces.

16

That afternoon, a little before four, we all piled into our VW van for the drive across town. The De Witts live in a big two-story house that seems to go on forever. Not fancy, but nice and so enormous I've never seen all the rooms.

We held the first class outside on the patio because of the size of the crowd. The clowns-to-be gathered at long redwood picnic tables. From folding chairs at one side, our mothers watched everything with great interest.

My sister Emily sat with some friends at the far table, much to my relief. In fact, with Nicole and Megan twittering with excitement, so pleased that all three of us had joined this class, I began to feel a mild enthusiasm myself.

Then Lorraine Foxworth came through the sliding glass door, and my heart descended to my toes. She doesn't like her first name, so everyone calls her Foxie, very appropriate since she's a tall zaftig blonde. She acts as though she likes me, but I'm always uneasy around her. She intimidates me somehow.

Foxie and I fell into a stupid pattern a couple years ago in junior high. I'd been crushed about losing out as cheerleader, even though everybody said it was nothing but a popularity contest. After all, if you're not loaded with talent, it isn't too comforting to know you aren't popular enough to make the grade, either. Anyway, I came up with a routine called The Cheerful Cheerleader—my way of chewing up a bunch of sour grapes. At the same time, I might divert people from the fact that I'd lost out on the real thing.

Foxie freaked out every time she saw that number, a hammy send-up of the way the girls did their stuff out on the field. Now, her eyes sparkled when she spotted me, and she came to park her big bouncing bod opposite us at the table.

"Hi, you guys. Might have known I'd find you here, Shelley. What kinda clown you gonna be? You figure you can use that cheerleader thing you do?"

I shrugged. "Nah. Too much trouble to shave my knees."

And then I cringed inside. One crack, usually mean, and I bounce off the walls like the village idiot. This time, Foxie hadn't even needled me, but I'd put myself down just the same. The whole dumb pattern repeats itself every time she comes around.

Last year, she invited me to a Halloween party, a dress-as-your-favorite-weirdo affair. She flashed all thirty-two teeth at me when she followed the invitation with the inevitable snapper: "Naturally, you'll come as yourself. Right, Shell?"

What did I do? Crossed my eyes, hung my top teeth out in a gopher grin, and cackled. Then hated myself for the rest of the day. Foxie, too.

That Tuesday, Mrs. De Witt helped restore my sagging spirits. She took up a position at the end of the next table, faced the mob, and whistled through her teeth for attention.

"Welcome." She smiled at us, a grown-up classier version of Dolly Dimples. I felt certain *she'd* been a cheerleader all through school. "You're in for a very interesting experience and a whole lot of fun," she said. "Everybody loves a clown. We love to laugh, don't we? Well, when people make us laugh—it's such a priceless gift—we love them, too. Now you're going to learn it's just as much fun to make others laugh as it is to laugh yourselves."

A buzz of conversation from Emily's table. I felt a prickle of annoyance and wished Mom hadn't chosen a seat so far from her.

Mrs. De Witt rapped on the table until the noise subsided. She went on to discuss a little of the history of clowning, much as we had done that night at the dinner table. She mentioned the clowns in Shakespeare—Feste in a play called *Twelfth Night* and the Fool in *King Lear*. Then she told us about the famous creation of a man named Joseph Grimaldi, a new clown "persona" he called Joey. Joey became more popular than the old harlequin clown of English pantomimes. To this day, he said, circus clowns are called "joeys" in Grimaldi's honor.

"A very famous mime today has chosen a modern

Pierrot character, a sad-faced clown you know as Bip. You've probably seen him on TV or on the stage. Can anybody tell me who created Bip?"

"I can! I know, Mrs. De Witt!" Emily, of course. "It's Marcel Marceau. And I could tell you about Henry VIII's fool, too. That was a man named William Somers and—"

Mrs. De Witt held up both hands. "You're right, Emily, and thanks a lot. But we can only sketch in a little of the history of clowns today. We have a lot to cover."

Megan nudged me, but didn't turn. I saw her slight smile in profile.

"Today clowns fall into three basic categories: the Whiteface, the Auguste, and the Tramp or Character clown, sometimes known as the Grotesque. That doesn't mean scary or repulsive makeup, however. How could a clown work in front of audiences with small children if there were anything about his appearance that might frighten them? Today's clowns certainly don't want to do that."

I heard Nicole sigh. She'd had her heart set on looking as ghastly as possible. It never occurred to any of us that little kids might be scared of a lady vampire or a witch with a big warty nose.

"We're going to put on the Whiteface makeup today," Mrs. De Witt told us. "Next week, the Auguste. And the week after that, the Tramp. You can choose then which type you want to be. Once you have your category set, you must come up with a name and a costume. Remember, everything should fit the clown you choose, the makeup and wig, too. One thing I want to stress right at the beginning. We are going into this in a professional way. You are going to be real clowns, not just little girls dressed up and acting silly. You'll learn everything you need to know at the beginning in this—"

Her voice disappeared beneath the rising wave of sound from my sister's table. I wanted to crawl under my own. I've never been sure about reincarnation, but it might explain a lot. I mean, if I was a real horror in a former lifetime, it's only right that I'm doing penance now with Emily.

Mom stood up and began to make her way through the rows of chairs, but before she got to Emily, Mrs. De Witt nailed her.

"Emily Lucas?" Her clear voice cut across my sister's. "Come on, babe. I'm the fearless leader around here. You just sit and pay attention, and someday you can teach the clown class. Okay?"

Everybody snickered, and Emily turned a dull red. She'll have to learn the hard way, I guess. By that time, her tonsils will be half their size, shriveled by all that hot air.

We settled down to business then, looking at the pictures Mrs. De Witt gave us of Whiteface clowns.

A couple of 4-H junior leaders who'd already had the class sat down to demonstrate the procedure. First, we pinned our hair back, then applied a cold-cream base so the makeup wouldn't go into the pores of our skin.

Nancy, our junior leader, showed us how to apply the Clown White, patting it on evenly. "You don't want any holidays," she said. "That's what they call bare or thin spots."

"Oh, I like this," Nicole crooned, dabbing on the white goo. She looked really strange, only her fantastic eyes offering a clue that the girl under the gunk was a beauty.

Also, the shyest, most insecure girl around. Not many people know why. Well, there were those first five years with the Ice Queen. Plus a real morale booster when Granny brought her home from Europe and her Mom never made a move to take her back.

Still, I think Nicole's real problems began in junior high with the boy-girl thing. Even now, the boys go into instant coma when she's around, or they get really obnoxious, showing off. Some of the girls detest her. Threatened, probably. Oh, there are others who are nice to her. But Meg and I are the only ones who truly know the girl behind the perfect face. A face she was doing her best to hide

22

right now behind the gaudy makeup of a clown.

Nancy told us, "You have to cover everything that your costume doesn't hide. Face, neck, ears. You even wear gloves."

"Now what?" Megan asked, giggling because I'd been making faces at her.

Mrs. De Witt paused on her tour of inspection to answer. "You powder it down to set it, to keep it from coming off." Her voice rose as she turned to address the rest. "This is one reason we're having the class outside, because the powder-down process makes such a mess. That's why the circus people insist that clowns stay in Clown Alley. Hold your breath while you're powdering, too. You don't want to breathe it."

We watched Nancy make goofy eyebrows with the black grease pencil and draw lines around her eyes. Then she used the red stuff to make an enormous mouth and little tears on her cheeks, carefully outlining the red areas with black.

"Oh, I've got to have a nose like that!" Megan exclaimed as she watched Nancy put it on, a little red ball with a few pearl buttons attached.

"What's your costume like?" I asked.

Nancy took some pictures from her bag, and everybody at the table laughed as we looked at them. Her costume was a baggy affair, a loose top and long skirt covered with buttons. With it she wore a frizzy wig and a hat. There were buttons sewed on that, too.

"Because of my name," Nancy said, smiling. "I'm Buttons. You see what Mrs. De Witt means about tying everything in? Name, costume, wig, and makeup. I can make jokes about my nose if I work with a partner. She says, 'You've got a button nose,' and I pretend to get mad and yell, 'No, you dummy, I've got buttons *on* my nose!' The sillier, the better for kids. Especially when they're little sick kids at the hospital."

Megan brightened. "That's the part I'd like," she said softly.

Meg loves kids. You'd think with a couple of pocket-size monsters in her own family that she'd be completely turned off, but she's even good with Riley and Tim. We tease her a lot about bucking for a halo.

Actually, all that saintliness with Riley and Tim makes me a little uneasy. It's as if she goes along with the general attitude in her family that her brothers are something special because they're so cute looking. She doesn't have much along that line going for her, tiny as she is and flat as a slat. Add that to lank hair, a blob of a nose, and a small thin-lipped mouth and you have Megan, the mouse. And

24

much much more if you aren't limited to the way somebody looks.

By the time we'd experimented with red and black designs on our white faces and studied the pages of noses and mouths that Mrs. De Witt passed around, the hour was up. We cleaned off the make-up with baby oil, packed our gear, and helped the junior leaders put the chairs away.

Back in the van, Nicole and Megan said they'd already decided they didn't want to be Whiteface clowns. That's a kind of slaphappy slapstick character, according to Mrs. De Witt. He gets into trouble because he's mischievous, but he's smart enough to get out of trouble again, too. She told us the Whiteface loves applause and hogs the spotlight in the circus until the ringmaster or some other performer practically drags him from the ring. Of course, it's all part of the act.

"I'd rather be a Tramp," Nicole said, "and wear beat-up clothes and huge shoes and crazy makeup. Like Wearie Willie or that famous one with Ringling Brothers. Emmett Kelly. Granny said he did a wonderful routine with a broom and dustpan, trying to sweep up the circle made by a spotlight on the arena floor. Of course they kept moving the light."

Emily piped up from the front seat, as if somebody had asked her. "My book said the Auguste always gets in trouble, too, because he's sort of a knucklehead. Everybody pushes him around. But he uses really neat props. Flowers that squirt or a tie that glows in the dark or—"

"I'd been thinking about that kind of character." Megan nodded. "Somebody that everybody picks on. The makeup makes him look really sad. Kids would like that sort of clown, don't you think?"

She poked me. "Shelley? Have you decided yet?"

I sighed. "Well, as long as they have three types, and there are three of us, why don't we all pick a different one? I'll go for the Whiteface. I can concentrate on what we did today and go ahead and get my costume together. I'm going to have enough to worry about with school coming up."

Nicole made a face. "You had to mention school, didn't you?"

"Come on," Megan soothed. "High school. It has to be better than junior high."

"Different," Nicole said crisply. "Not necessarily better."

We talked about school until we got home. Nicole is antsy about meeting people, and any kind of change bothers her a lot. I was a little tense about the idea of high school, too, but not as paranoid as Nicole.

Looking back, I'm certain that Megan was the only one who felt pure terror. If Nicole's insecure, Meg's inadequate—in her own view, of course. She

26

looks about twelve. There's nothing especially cute or appealing about her size. She's just little. If that meant dumb, condescending cracks in junior high—and it had—it might be worse in high school.

She probably was scared, all right, but she never let on. In my opinion, that's true courage. Nicole and I work off a lot of steam bitching about things, freaking out over the little stuff. Megan meets everything head-on, with the same set smile. Sometimes she fools me, until I touch her hand and discover that it's cold and clammy.

When we came in our drive after dropping everybody off, Jon Harrington waved from across the hedge. He takes care of the flower beds for his mother because she has something wrong with her back. She adores flowers, and they're planted all around the borders of both lawns, even at the base of the big tree in front. It means he spends a lot of time outside.

I make a lot of excuses to spend time in the yard when Jon's there. That afternoon, the minute we'd unpacked the car, I closed the garage door and wandered over to get the paper from where the boy always throws it—under the rail fence by the side of the driveway. Once in a while I give him fifty cents to keep it coming in the same spot.

He's a little wimp with big sad eyes that always look a little alarmed, maybe because he's not sure

I'm playing with a full deck. But he hits the target with the evening paper, just the same. Who's going to argue with fifty-cent tips, even when they come from a real fruit loop?

Jon looked up and grinned. He has red hair and freckles and green eyes, but not the wild and crazy personality that sometimes goes with vivid coloring like that. He's very laid back, as a matter of fact, so I'm not as hyper as usual around him.

"How was the clown class?" he asked.

"How'd you know about it?"

He lifted his sensational shoulders. "The Word Factory." It's his name for Emily. Not to her face, though.

"You know, I dragged my feet about this class," I told him, "but it's actually kind of interesting. In fact, I may be good at clowning."

Jon laughed. "I wouldn't be a bit surprised." He stood up and stretched. Then he hit me with a stunning line. "Shelley, the day you stop going for yucks, you'll find out you're good at a whole lot of things."

Just then, his mother stuck her head out the door to call him to the phone, so I didn't have a chance to ask him what he meant.

It must have stung clear down to my subconscious, though, because I dreamed about Jon that night. He was doing an Emmett Kelly number, trying to sweep up the spotlight with a tattered broom. When he moved, following the light, I could see a picture in the center of that circle. A Whiteface clown.

Somehow, I knew it was a picture of me.

3

The three of us went down to the shopping centers almost every day for a week, getting things for our costumes. Mrs. De Witt told us the code word was KISS—Keep It Simple, Stupid—and that we should emphasize creativity, putting an outfit together inexpensively and with imagination. That meant hitting the thrift shops, Goodwill, and the places run by disabled veterans.

Nicole and Megan wanted big floppy coats and pants that they could turn into clown suits with patches here and there. We would need pockets to carry balloons and whatever props we needed for magic tricks.

They both had instant success. Megan got a black coat three sizes too large and a pair of pants in a traffic-stopping color, more orange than peach. Nicole found something even gaudier, a green-checked jacket with red plaid slacks. By the time we left the store, the manager, two clerks, and all the customers had entered into the spirit of hilarity.

Megan giggled all the way to Mac's, where we restored our energy with burgers and shakes. "Shelley, we have to decide on something for you now. You're going to be a Whiteface, but what're you going to *do*?"

"Be myself," I said airily. "That's always good for a few laughs."

"Come on," Nicole said, "be serious. You must have some idea for a routine. Balloons'd be fun. We're going to learn how to make animals with them, poodles and dachshunds and stuff."

"More in Emily's line," I said. "Old Leather Lungs. Those long balloons are hard to blow up."

"You can use a pump." Megan grinned and pointed her straw at me. "I know. Card tricks. You're good at those."

We all caught fire with the idea, forgetting to eat for at least three minutes as we enlarged on it. We came up with a name for a Whiteface clown who does card tricks: Acey Deucey. My costume would be a turtleneck and a vest and pants in a neutral

31

color. I could sew on colored cutouts of spades and diamonds and hearts and clubs.

"Hey, I could put those on my face, too," I said, feeling really good now that things were falling into line. "Little hearts and diamonds instead of the tears that Nancy made. And I wouldn't have to do card tricks all the time. I could just say to people, 'Take a card, any card,' and they'd be slips of paper with jokes or riddles."

Nicole laughed. "Like the ones you used to give Miss Crawford in sixth grade. Every time she turned her back, you put a new one on her desk. Took her two months to catch you."

"And the Funny Phonics! And your Foul Vowels!" Megan grinned. "Haven't thought of those in years. How did they go?"

All I could remember were the Foul Vowels. The Funny Phonics were big on the chart in seventh grade when my sense of humor was as immature as the rest of me.

A What people say when they want you to speak louder.

E What you say when you see a mouse.

I An exclamation girls use when a fantastic guy walks by (usually followed by 2 extra syllables, as in *I-yi-yi*)

O   Generally preceded by another word in a derogatory expression: *weird-o, boz-o, flak-o*

U   The opposite of *I*. Can also precede *hoo* when you're trying to get someone's attention.

Y   Used as a question when your parents ask you to do something dumb like clean up your room.

My only comment on our sense of humor these days is that we broke up all over again, not much more sophisticated than we were three years ago.

After I got home, I went through the bag where Mom puts old clothes to give to the Salvation Army. Sure enough, she'd discarded a tan pantsuit. Some little cherub at the school where she works had made a big mark on one sleeve and the back with a black felt pen. It'd be a cinch to make a vest out of it, and I could sew a cutout over the mark on the back.

On the Monday before the second clown class, we spent the whole afternoon at Nicole's working on our costumes. Megan and I still had the wigs we used to wear for Halloween. Mine, a short red one that I combed straight out from my head. Hers, a black curly affair. Both of them were little cheapies from Penney's. Nicole had one that her grandmother donated, expensive and glamorous compared to ours.

That day, Granny Gus, a tiny little birdlike lady, sat on the couch by the window. The sun shone on her gray hair, which she wears in a cute flippy ponytail tied with a black velvet ribbon.

Nicole sat on the floor with Megan and me, examining the cap of elegant gray curls perched on her knee. "Granny, it's such a beautiful wig. Are you sure you won't wear it again?"

Granny Gus made a face. "I never have worn it," she said briskly. "But don't tell your mother. When she gave up trying to get me to do something with my hair, she brought me that."

Her eyes sparkled with laughter. "The way I look at it, a person my age is entitled to be a little eccentric. You go through life trying to please other people, first your parents, then your husband. Even the neighbors, for pity's sake. When I realized my *daughter* was—" She paused. "What's the expression you girls use? A polite term for bullying?"

"She was on your case," Nicole said gently, smoothing a gray curl around one finger. "Every minute."

Granny chuckled. "I've been a great disappointment to Wanda," she said. "But I must say, I never had any fun at all until I quit trying to be a silk purse. I'll be a sow's ear from here on out. It's much more restful."

Nicole patted the small foot in its ridiculous red tennie swinging in midair beside her shoulder. Granny Gus favors tennies, or patent leather shoes with flat heels and straps like the ones little girls wear to Sunday School. More restful, probably.

"You're just perfect," Nicole said, her voice firm. "Who wants a dumb silk purse around the house?"

I looked up from the red cloth diamond I was sewing onto my clown vest and saw Granny's expression as she stared at Nicole's bent head. She looked so sad that it startled me, and I jabbed the needle into my thumb. That meant I had to stop and suck the wound because I always bleed like crazy. I may be short on beauty and brains, but I sure have lots of blood.

Anyway, that's how I happened to be watching when they touched on a subject that clearly bothered both of them. Maybe I'd heard them talk about it before, but I hadn't noticed their faces, so it hadn't made any impression.

"You spoil me." Granny smiled, but her small face still looked as if she were close to tears. "And Tilly spoils me. When I go to the Sunnyside Home, those nice people will go right on spoiling me. I must say—"

"You aren't going anywhere, Gran! I wish you'd stop talking about that place." Nicole's lips tightened like they always do when she's upset.

"It's a lovely home. I'm sure you'd agree if you saw it. And it occurs to me that's one place they'll take you to practice clowning. To the children's ward in the hospital, of course. And out to Sunnyside."

"Thanks for the warning. I'll skip that trip."

I exchanged a glance with Megan. The harsh note in Nicole's voice had alerted her, too, to strange vibes in this conversation.

Granny sighed. "Nicky, I'd like some tea," she said. "I'll bet the girls could use some refreshments, too. Would you please ask Tilly—?"

"Sure." In one quick movement, Nicole was on her feet.

When she left the room, Granny Gus leaned forward. "Shelley, Megan, I want to ask you a favor. Can you get her to go on that trip out to Sunnyside?"

"Uh—we'll try," I said.

"Sure," Megan agreed, sounding as uncertain as I did. "We'll do our best."

Granny nodded and leaned back. "This tricky heart of mine," she said. "In case it acts up again, the doctor wants me where I'd get care right away.

He's getting stubborn about it." A ghost of a smile. "You might say he's on my case."

"And Nicole—she doesn't like the idea." I'd seen that for myself, so I wasn't asking a question, just stating a fact.

"Nicole won't discuss it. She hasn't even bothered to get her driver's license to make it easier to drive out to see me. It's a case of—not facing the inevitable." Granny suddenly looked much older.

I knew it was also a case of a person who hated anything new in her life. Nicole'd been through a lot of upheaval when she was little. The messy divorce, her father's death a few years later. Granny Gus and Tilly were the only adults she felt she could count on. It wasn't any wonder that she dreaded the thought of losing her grandmother. When Granny went into that nursing home, Nicole would face the most drastic change in the last ten years of her life.

Tilly and Nicole came in with a tray, and we switched to a safer topic, our costumes. Tilly is larger and rounder than Granny, a rosy cheerful person. She sat down to help Nicole sew a few patches on her outfit, in solid bright colors so they'd show against the lurid patterns.

"You'll sure be a sight," Tilly said, smiling. "Pretty girls like you, all working hard to look just terrible.

That's the most comical thing I ever heard of."

Tilly would have been even more amused had she attended class the next day. Nine of us had put our outfits together and worn them to the session as Mrs. De Witt had asked.

Almost everyone had some idea about the kind of clown they wanted to be. Several of them had come up with a name: Swirls, Polka Dotty, Pom-Pom, Frizzy, and Sneezer. Megan had chosen the name Patches, and Nicole would be Bubble Bum.

True to her image, Foxie came as Big Mama with lots of padding fore and aft in her costume, as if nature hadn't already bountifully blessed her.

She checked me out with great interest and the throaty laugh that turns the guys into zombies. Naturally, it was wasted on a bunch of girls, but I suppose she has to practice on somebody.

"Hey, Shell, that—is—*you*," she said. Then, predictably, came the zinger. "Of course, with your hokey image, you've got it made. In spades," she added, poking one of the cutouts on my vest.

"Ho ho ho." I had to work for the lame comeback. The two of us may finish school on this same high plane.

Everybody loved the props that Megan and Nicole brought. They'd found a store that carried magician supplies and a lot of clown stuff, too. Nicole got a big pipe with a pink flower sticking out of the clay in the bowl. Megan bought a derby that had a daisy growing out the top. My pitiful allowance wouldn't stretch to cover any extras for at least six months, so I'd passed up that shopping expedition, afraid I'd be tempted.

Mom had talked to Emily about yakking so much in class. She must have made a few points because I didn't hear a chirp out of Cricket until the end of the hour. Her clown name sure fits her. Crickets are forever sounding off, too.

That afternoon we experimented with the Auguste face: a big white mouth, white around the eyes. Red on cheeks, brow, and nose and on the upper lip above the white outline. Then, with a liner brush, a black line around the mouth and soaring eyebrows. The beard applied with a stipple brush. Last, the powder-down process.

Mrs. De Witt told us, "When you're going to perform and it looks like a long session, you'll want to set your makeup so it'll last. You do that by dipping a sponge in cold water, wringing it dry, and pressing it to your face."

She passed around her big 4-H scrapbook to show us Auguste faces. Those pictures meant more to us today, because we were aware now of all the work that went into the development of a clown persona.

There were no two alike. Mrs. De Witt explained the unwritten rule among clowns: The first one to come up with a certain face has an unofficial copy-right on it. She suggested we follow that guideline, as well.

Everybody went along except for a couple of fifth-graders who both had the bright idea of copying the makeup on a full-page picture in the scrapbook. Jan-Ellen and Brenda both have small faces with sharp features, so they ended up looking like midget clones.

Just before they reached the hair-pulling stage, Mrs. De Witt suggested they flip a coin. Brenda, the sore loser, turned the page and swiped another professional image. She said shrilly that it didn't make a bit of difference. The pro clowns were so old, they must all be dead by now.

Mrs. De Witt rolled her eyes. "You think they're decrepit? They could be younger than I am. Ah well, you girls keep me humble. Who knows? It may lead to a fifth H. The 5-H clubs. Does that have a ring to it? Head, heart, hands, health and—the big-gie reserved for us leaders—humility." She walked away muttering something about early senility.

"Grow up!" I snapped at Brenda, sore because she'd hurt Mrs. De Witt's feelings.

When I realized what I'd said, I didn't open my mouth again for a whole half hour. It happens to be something I hate, the way people are forever saying "Grow up!" to kids. As if you could do it in a flash if you put your mind to it.

Byron snarls at me a lot, "Grow up, willya!" There's absolutely nothing you can say to a put-down like that. Think about it. What's he saying? That I'm *not* grown up yet? Right, I'm fifteen. Is it my fault I'm not fully mature? Neither is Byron.

It really upset me, hearing his words come out of my mouth. I'd hoped the maturing process wouldn't change me into the kind of insensitive nerd who says things like "Grow up!" to kids who are the age I am now. I often promise myself I'll write all these things down so I won't forget. But I never do.

It's vaguely comforting to know he doesn't read me any better than I can read him, though I have to admit he surprises me more. Always Mr. Cool when it comes to showing what he feels, so it's usually a shock when I find out.

Our conversation that night was a good example. I had just put together a snack to hold me until bedtime. Closing the refrigerator door, I found Byron leaning against the sink, arms folded, staring at me.

"Hey, Shell, how old is Nicole?"

"Almost sixteen."

"Mmmm-hmmmm. When?"

"December first."

"Uh-huh. Does she date at all?" His eyes were intent beneath the thick bristling brows so much like Dad's. Byron has the scar, of course, a fascinating interruption of the left eyebrow just at the peak. He touches that scar gently when he talks. Maybe it's an unconscious gesture, but I doubt it. Byron pushes all the right buttons. It's as if he came equipped with a how-to manual when he was born.

"No, Nicole doesn't date much," I said obscurely. I knew Nicole doesn't go to anything but boy-girl parties, and only the kind where they invite singles, not couples. But I wasn't about to tell Byron that.

He pursued the subject while I pretended indifference. I don't know why his obvious interest jolted me. Nicole is exceptionally pretty, and my brother's eyesight is as perfect as everything else about his fabulous body. Nicole must be well aware of his great looks, popularity, and football hero reputation. Still, I simply couldn't imagine those two as A Couple.

"You think she'll date now she's in high school?"

"I wouldn't be surprised," I said. "Unless all the guys at Mesa Vista suddenly go blind by next Monday morning. God forbid," I added piously.

Byron gave me a full-voltage smile. I pretended to stagger back under the impact, shielding my eyes like Dracula abruptly confronted with the symbol of goodness and purity. It's a little number that always infuriates Byron, so he ends up yelling at me.

That night was no exception. "Nobody can talk to you for three minutes before you do your weird little tapdance. *Why don't you grow up?*"

4

Mesa Vista isn't a big town. It's what they call a bedroom community. My Dad says that means everybody works somewhere else, and that's good in a way, not having factories and smoke and smog.

The words "bedroom community" give me a weird image, though. I picture a place with nothing but single rooms joined together in long, long rows. All of them are bedrooms, and there's no sound anywhere but a steady *zzzzzzzz* from all the sleepers.

That would be a whole lot more interesting than the way it really is, just another southern California suburb with stucco or frame houses in the old part of town, ranch houses and condos or big two-story places in the newer section. The shopping malls are mostly on the outskirts, because Mesa Vista dates way back to the early part of the century.

The kids from our area go to a high school within walking distance. It's one that's gone back to a four-year plan because there are fewer students now.

That Monday morning in September I went by to pick up Megan, as usual. A few blocks later Nicole joined us on the corner of the street where they've built about a dozen condos. Despite all her gloomy comments, Nicole seemed as excited about our first day of high school as we were. I guess we were all a little scared, too.

Megan said right away, "I couldn't eat one bite of breakfast. It's a good thing Mom was going crazy trying to get my brothers out of bed. She didn't notice."

It figured, I thought. Megan could starve to death before anybody in her family noticed she'd gone down to ribs and anklebones.

"Do I look okay?" she asked, sounding anxious.

Nicole stopped to study her, then handed me her bag to hold. "Give me your comb, okay?" She parted Megan's hair in the middle, then fluffed out the sides and bangs and looked at me. "What do you think?"

"Looks great. Megan, you should put her on the payroll."

"Thanks," she said. "I'll die if I don't get you guys in some of my classes. I need a transfusion every so often. Confidence, not blood."

I laughed. "Relax. You'll be in Advisory with me if they go alphabetically. Lucas, Malloncrodt—"

Nicole groaned. "And Baldridge will be out in the cold. I hope I get one of you in Math or Spanish or English or—" Her eyes widened. "I've gone blank. What's the other class?"

"History."

"Yeah," she said. "You know what Nancy told me last week at 4-H? The P.E. teachers are worse than in junior high. Can you believe that?"

"They breed them on another planet." I sounded grim. That's how P.E. teachers affect me. It's been my experience that they're either Molly Marines or Smilers.

There must be thousands of girls in this country who absolutely love P.E. and the women who teach it. At least, that's what I keep telling myself. Truth is, I've only met about six girls who fit in that category. They are all perfectly coordinated, bursting with health and bulging muscles that do anything required of them.

There must be lots of reasons that people like Nicole and Megan and me drift together and form lasting friendships. One of them has to be a law of nature that can be observed in every P.E. class in the nation. Born athletes bound to the head of the line, any line at all, and the klutzes huddle in a corner, hoping desperately to be overlooked. When you're a kid, there can't be anything more miserable than waiting while a couple of girl jocks choose teams to play some dumb game. They never do call your name. When everybody else is lined up, one of them just gets stuck with you.

"A Molly Marine might be a welcome change," Megan said, "after two years of Smiley Norton." She did a fair imitation of the teacher we had last year. "'Come on, girls, we're going to build healthy haaaappy bodies. Ten push-ups to start and then—'" She shuddered.

I had to agree. Around the cheerful Smilers, my toenails curl. "Still," I said, "I bet there isn't much difference between the Smiley ones and the lady drill-instructors. Molly Marines say the same thing, just in different words. 'Come on, girls, get the lead out. Ten push-ups to start and then—'" We talked about that the rest of the way to school.

Actually, P.E. doesn't bother me too much anymore, maybe a four on the Downer scale. Organized sports never add much joy to my day. I am so uncoordinated, you'd think I dedicated every waking moment to preserving my image as a knuckle-toed nerd—stubbed toes, black-and-blue hipbones, the whole shot. But I don't waste energy worrying about it.

That Monday, we'd have a minimum day. That means thirty-five-minute classes, just long enough to get sorted out. The teachers would be trying to size us up while they explained the material we'd cover during the year. We'd be making notes on them, too, figuring out which ones were marking time to retirement, and zeroing in on the hard cases who demanded a certain amount of work for a grade and accepted no excuses.

There would be others who might be cunningly diverted from planned lectures to a discussion of baseball or whatever their particular enthusiasm might be. There must be lots of kids like me who consider ourselves fortunate to find a few nuggets, teachers who make their classes interesting and who really care about us. Somebody watches over me. I've had a lot of nuggets in my time.

At the end of that day, however, I couldn't be sure I'd lucked out this year. Miss Adams, the English teacher, was little and plump and giggly. She'd even go for something off-the-wall like my Foul Vowels. I could have her in my pocket, no sweat, except for one thing. Jon Harrington not only landed in that class, he sat right behind me.

48

"This way I can keep an eye on you," he said.

"You just made my day." I grinned to myself when he laughed. It's funny how you can tell people the complete and total truth, and they think you're kidding. Jon couldn't hear my heart going *vroom-vroom* as if it were getting ready to burst through my chest and take off for the stars.

He turned up in my next class, too, and I began to wonder if somebody was trying to tell me something. Like, "This year, kid, you get a break."

Megan bounced into the seat behind me, glowing with pleasure because we had the same history class. So Jon took the seat in front, turning just once to say, "You get equal time."

Ten seconds later, Megan flipped a note over my shoulder. It was brief. "What did he *say?*"

I made my reply equally terse. "Tell you later."

The History teacher fascinated me, a tall bony man with a classic voice-from-the-tomb. I wondered if he'd ever studied to be a Shakespearean actor. Had he decided to settle for a job that would give him three square meals a day? He looked so skinny, I doubted he'd been getting that many. Maybe he had a dozen kids.

Nicole came into my fifth-period Spanish class, and we fell on each other as if we'd been separated for months.

49

"I don't know one single person in English," she wailed. "And nobody in History but Foxie. She'll just sit and sneer at me all year."

She was probably right about that. Nicole seems to threaten the Big Mama type. It seems so unnecessary. Dazzling girls like Nicole and sexpots like Foxie will eventually divide up almost all the boys around. If I can swallow hard and accept that fact, why can't Foxie? She won't be hurting for dates. It'll be people like me who'll have to scrounge for leftovers.

I may be open and honest about that, but it's not a matter of being a good sport. I never am. Sure, I grit my teeth and smile and congratulate all the Foxies around, but deep down inside I'm hoping it's the last good thing that ever happens to them. Maybe somebody will find out the truth someday: There aren't any good sports around, only hypocrites with a lot of acting ability.

Nicole and I settled back in a corner to listen to Mrs. Kramer, a tall dark woman with a mouth that looked as if she'd been sucking on a green persimmon. I amused myself by making up a whole bio to explain her bitter expression: She'd been raised in foster homes where she had to work like a slave. Then she ran away to get married, and the guy turned out to be a bigamist with two other wives and six kids.

I ended up feeling so sorry for her I gave her a radiant smile as I followed Nicole out of the room. Maybe it made Mrs. Kramer feel better. More likely she just figured me for another smack.

Nicole and I had the same P.E. class, too. We got a Molly Marine, Mrs. Upjohn. She looked like a Smiler to me at first. Anybody with deep dimples is going to exercise them a lot. But the minute she told us we'd begin each class by jogging around the track, I knew. She might look like a Smiler on the outside, but inside there beat the cast-iron heart of a Molly Marine.

I'd already decided the only unique thing about that class might be the gross jokes about the teacher's name. In fact, I'd begun to feel a certain compassion for the lady, but it vanished in the echo of her announcement about the once-around-the-track warm-up. As a result, it wasn't necessary to give myself a lecture about going soft and soppy about two teachers in a row. I should have known. The thing about Molly Marines is, they're consistent. Hardhearted, ruthless, sadistic. Depend on it.

I went into my last class, Math, with a black cloud directly overhead, which the teacher did nothing to dispel. Mr. Marion turned out to be stocky, stern, humorless. If you've ever noticed, people who are good at math are seldom comedians. There's nothing remotely amusing about the subject, of course.

51

You don't substitute one figure or angle or equation for another just for laughs.

The deadly part about math is that nothing ever changes. That makes me nervous. Maybe it's because my life is flawed, and often my only consolation is in knowing it won't stay this way. There's at least a small chance it will get better.

After Math, Nicole met Megan and me at our lockers and we walked home, dissecting the day. Conclusion: Our first year in high school would not be as bad as we'd feared. On the other hand, it would not be as good as we'd prayed it might be.

It seemed to me it wouldn't be much different from junior high. Bigger school, harder classes, but everything else pretty much the same. I could find only one thing about Mesa Vista High worthy of a rave notice. I'd be seeing Jon in two classes every day. I could watch him and enjoy the little fantasies I'd been building since the day he moved in next door. Over and over, I'd rescue him from flaming buildings, from dogs gone berserk, or from the paths of runaway trucks. If that got boring after a while, I'd change the script so he rescued *me*. I didn't share my journey to cloudland with Nicole or Megan. I can't discuss the way I feel about Jon even with them.

Before we separated at Nicole's corner, we made plans for the next day. We were to dress in our clown outfits and meet at Mrs. De Witt's for the class. Then we'd all go to Mac's for dinner. None of us had our skits ready or any of the tricks for our regular routines. Before we learned that sort of thing, Mrs. De Witt wanted us to see a professional clown, Blinko, who would perform next week. Dinner at Mac's would be *our* first appearance in public, and we were all curious about what people would say or do when we trooped in, wearing full makeup and the costumes we'd created.

Ten minutes after I got in the house, the phone rang.

"Are you alone?" Nicole asked urgently.

"Yeah. Byron's at football practice and Emily hasn't checked in yet. She's still counting ants on the way home from school, I suppose. It's been a big year for ants, so—"

"Are you in your room with the extension and the door closed?"

"Yeah, matter of fact. I'm lying on my bed eating an apple. A Golden Delicious that's slightly overripe, and I have about three bites left and—"

"Shell—*eeee!*"

I said huffily, "Well, you seemed to want all the details. I was just filling in the total picture."

"Listen, Shell, this is serious."

"Oh. Well, why didn't you say so? What's happening?"

She sighed. "What's happening is so unreal, I don't believe it. It's your brother. It's Byron."

Aha. I almost said that aloud, but caught myself in time. I should have realized from Nicole's breathless voice that she'd hit the panic button, even though she hadn't given me a clue on the way home from school. Still, I'd been wandering in and out of my Jon-and-Shelley scenarios, and I might not have picked up on anything unusual.

Nicole was silent, so I offered a casual comment. "Yeah, Byron asked me about you the other day."

"He did? What did he want to know?"

I hesitated, torn between two separate loyalties. I didn't see how it could hurt to tell the truth. Besides, Nicole had never dated before, and Byron had the benefit of a couple years' experience. It seemed only fair that I level with her.

"He just asked me how old you are and if you date."

"Oh, Shell, what'd you tell him?"

"I said you didn't date much."

"That's exactly what you said?"

"That is precisely what I said."

"That's good."

I could hear her breathing, but nothing else except the last faint notes of "I'll Never Fall in Love Again" in the background. I can't remember whose recording it is. Nicole has had it for ages and she plays it constantly. Sure, the song's okay, but I wouldn't think it would have any meaning for somebody who's never *been* in love.

Nicole said at last, "Well—"

I waited.

"Byron came by my locker just before last period and—"

I waited some more.

"He asked if I'd be going to the first game." Another pause. "And—if I wanted to go out afterward."

I thought about several things I might say, canceled them all, and settled for "Mmmm-hmmm."

Apparently, I'd hit on a brilliant summation of the situation, because Nicole talked for several minutes without pausing for breath. The bottom line was that she'd decided she had to start dating *sometime*, and it seemed as if the brother of one of her friends would be *safe*, and she knew Byron a little bit already, and he didn't scare her out of her mind like *some* guys did, and—"What do you think, Shell?"

By this time, I was lying flat on my back, my bare feet in the air, with the vague theory that the blood would thereby flow to my head. That would stimulate my brain, making it possible to handle this thing tactfully.

I addressed my toes. "It's very difficult to be objective about my own brother, Nico, but I'll give it a shot." After that, I listed the opinion of the community at large about Byron Lowell Lucas, and spared her my personal view.

"Everybody says he has wonderful manners." *Around the house, he acts like a cross between King Kong and Cro-Magnon man.* "He's good-looking and he dresses pretty well." *And anybody who clocks him can tell you it takes this dude two hours to get ready for a big evening.* "But the main thing is, he concentrates on one girl." *One at a time, that is.*

My halo began to pinch a little, but I threw in a last bouquet. "When he breaks up with someone, they stay friends with him. I can think of at least two girls who call him once in a while just to rap or ask his advice or something. Even though they're going with someone else."

Nicole said after a moment, "That's—kind of unusual, isn't it?"

I had to agree. Not that I've had any experience along that line, but the people I know seem to break up with a lot of yelling and hollering, everything short of a shooting war.

"He seems nice," Nicole said softly. "I don't think I've ever known anybody named Byron."

"Yup, one of a kind." I told her how the kids in grammar school reacted to his unusual name, with lots of snickering and hooting after him. "Is it *My*ron or *Ty*ron or *Ly*ron? No, it's *By*ron!" Then some little

56

rat heard the teacher say there was a poet named Lord Byron. So they started calling him Lord.

"Wow." Nicole giggled. "What did he do?"

"Probably punched their lights out. He'd come home every day with his shirt ripped. And so sweaty and grimy, it looked as if he'd wrestled with somebody all over the playground. Not a mark on him, otherwise, so Mom and Dad just raised their eyebrows and pretended to go along with the stories he handed out. After a while, no more problems. At least, nothing physical. Little kids can be mean. You know?"

"Yeah," she said. "I know."

After we hung up, I went out to the kitchen to find Emily fixing her afterschool snack. She's into sandwiches with yucky mixtures like cranberry sauce and peanut butter. Maybe she thinks she'll stumble across something sensational nobody else has thought about, and it'll make her rich and famous. Today's combo, sliced bananas and mayonnaise on rye, would not be a winner. I watched her dubious expression as she ate and laughed to myself. One thing you have to say about Emily, she doesn't cry over her mistakes. She eats them like a little soldier.

"Byron's got a new girl," she announced. Her big gray eyes sparkled.

She went on for five minutes as I perched on the kitchen stool, wondering if I could interest the FBI

57

in Emily and her hotline. She's developed a spy network that's so efficient she hears the news the same day it happens. She's annoyed if she doesn't get the total scoop within an hour. She usually does. Sometimes, it's downright spooky.

Her monologue that day came down to: "It's a friend of yours. For fifty cents, I'll tell you who."

"Deal."

She grinned, naked greed in those lovely luminous eyes. "Nicole Baldridge."

"Saints alive," I said.

She extended a small sticky paw. "Pay up."

I looked at her. "On the other hand," I said, "it should be worth at least a dollar to you if I keep my mouth shut. Byron will not be thrilled to hear that you're blatting this bulletin all over town—even before his first date with Nicole."

Emily's mouth opened, but only one strangled sound emerged. Something like "Urrrk—"

"I'll settle for fifty cents," I said. "So we're even."

She wouldn't speak to me for the next two hours. I hate to descend to her level this way, but it's time she learned that crime doesn't pay.

And, in her case, a snitch won't get rich, either.

5

Sometimes you can look back and see that a particular incident has been a kind of milestone in your life. Still, you almost never know at the time that it's important. You have to figure out first what you learned from it, and that can take a while.

On the day our clown class went to Mac's, several things happened to me in rapid succession. All I can say is, it's a wonder my brain didn't overload and blow a few vital circuits.

Up to seventh period, it had been business as usual, beginning with Advisory when the teacher yelled at Megan and me for talking. English and History would have been deadly if Jon hadn't been in the same room. If fantasy can be considered ed-ucational, I'm in great shape. During Spanish, Mrs. Kramer threatened to separate Nicole and me if we didn't stop talking so much. An ordinary day, as I say.

After P.E., given the opportunity, I'd have hopped off and let the world go on without me. As always, I failed to distinguish myself in the areas of skill, coordination, and grace. I fell on the track during warm-up and lacerated my knee. Then I gave a performance in volleyball that was even more dis-mal than usual.

I am no better at golf or baseball or tennis. There simply is no meaningful contact between me and any ball in play, whether I'm swinging a club, bat, or racket, or grabbing wildly for it with my bare hands, as I did that afternoon. Where the ball was, I was not. Worse, I hit it and sent it in the wrong direction. My teammates screamed at me furiously all during that terrible game.

An eternity later, Mrs. Upjohn sent the cheering winners and the muttering losers off to the showers. I lagged behind, pretending to tie my shoes, and I heard another tweet from her whistle.

"Lucas? See you a minute?"

Fantastic. Just what I needed, an analysis of my flaws. Well, why not look on the bright side? If she did a thorough job, it could last halfway through Math class.

The rest of us had ended up red-faced and sweating, but Mrs. Upjohn looked totally gorgeous, every blond hair in place. It never fails to mystify me, because she's one P.E. teacher who's an active participant in our games.

"Lucas," she said, her smile as cool and attractive as the rest of her, "you're having a few problems." The understatement of the century.

I nodded. Actually, my throat was so tight, speech would have been impossible. I felt like a bumbling, butterfingered blob, unlovely and unloved.

"Listen," Mrs. Upjohn said, "eye-hand coordination doesn't come overnight. At your age, every cell in your body is changing. Doesn't make any difference how old you are or how tall you are. It takes *time* to mature fully, and it's not necessarily the same amount of time for any two people. Everyone develops physical skills on a unique schedule."

I sighed and relaxed a little, staring at her adorable dimples and trying not to hate her. I read somewhere that hate and anger can chew up your insides, and I don't want to die before I'm old enough for a driver's license.

"You can try a few things that might help," she

said. "Bouncing a tennis ball with a racket or hitting it against a garage door. Working out with a jump rope. Swimming, dancing—I have a theory that anything that involves body rhythm improves coordination, too."

"You mean—if I practice outside class, I'll stop falling over my feet?"

Mrs. Upjohn didn't laugh until I did. "The girls gave you a rough time today. But you seem to be popular. Nice outgoing personality—no problem there."

She studied me. "Give yourself another year, maybe six months, and you'll be one of the most striking-looking girls at school, too. Don't get impatient just because you're not quite at the end of the assembly line." The dimples flickered once more. "You have limitless potential, Lucas. When you get it together, it's going to be some package."

She nodded, tapped my arm, and jogged toward the office, leaving me staring after her in a state of shock. How could I have been so far off target when I first sized her up? Why, she saw possibilities in me that I never dreamed existed.

Potential. The wonderful word buzzed around inside, leaving a warm healing balm in its wake. Mrs. Upjohn had given me a priceless gift, hope for the future. Inside this bumbling, butterfingered blob,

a terrific person waited to emerge, someone grace-
ful and poised and—my cup filled up and slopped
over—*striking looking*.

I went to take my shower, ignoring the snide
comments that came from my sorehead teammates
as I trotted through the locker room. Standing under
the warm water, I happily recast my old fantasy so
I could rescue Mrs. Upjohn from flaming buildings,
dogs gone berserk, and out of the paths of runaway
trucks. Had Jon been written into the same script,
I'm sure I could have saved him, as well.

My heart expanded as I marveled at my new
discovery: Sometimes even Molly Marines turn out
to be nuggets.

*I love you madly, Mrs. Upjohn. I shall destroy the next
scumbag who calls you Mrs. Upchuck.*

I smiled all during Math class. Mr. Marion came
back at the end of the period, his stern face almost
soft with concern. "You feeling okay, Shelley? Running a fever? Your face is so flushed, I thought—"

I'd never suspected there could be anything beneath his granite exterior but more granite. I beamed
at him, happy to be proven wrong a second time.

"No, I feel great, Mr. Marion. I just came from
P.E."

"Ah." He almost smiled, but not quite. The poor
thing must be rusty from lack of practice. "Tennis?"

"Volleyball."

He preceded me up the aisle. "You look so happy, your team must have won big."

"No," I said over my shoulder on my way to the door. "Actually, we got whomped." At my locker later, my euphoria disappearing, I grinned as I realized how that must have confused him.

When I got home from school, the scene at our house was pretty chaotic. Emily and I had to change into costume, get our makeup on, and be ready to leave by four-thirty for Mrs. De Witt's. Somehow we made it out the door in a matter of seconds after we heard Mrs. Malloncrodt's car in the drive.

I collapsed in the backseat, realizing now why Mrs. De Witt stressed the importance of simplicity. She had urged us to come up with a costume that would be comfortable, easy to get on and off, not too warm, and one that had lots of pockets. Our clown faces should be easy, too, so we could put them on quickly.

Emily had taken her advice. She could do her Cricket makeup in a fast twenty minutes. She'd limited herself to whiteface, swooping eyebrows, a little red on the tip of her nose and a big red mouth. My face took twice as long because I used more black lines and a red heart and diamond on my cheeks.

By this time, almost everyone in class had added the final touches to their costumes. There were all

64

kinds of wigs in every conceivable color. Bushy, curly wigs, straight-haired ones arranged in wild disarray, expensive acrylic wigs, and simple ones made from mopheads. Emily had one with bangs and braids made of yarn that she wore under a baseball cap.

I think we showed even more imagination in the shoes we chose. There were a few tennies and ballet shoes, but almost all the clowns had been more creative, making colorful fuzzy shoes from bedroom slippers or transforming huge workshoes with bright paint. Several girls wore Adidas inside much larger shoes decorated with paint or polka dots, colored laces, and pompons.

That's what I decided to do after I talked Byron out of an old pair of tennis shoes. It worked out fine. He has enormous feet. In fact, if he had a brain in proportion to his shoe size, his I.Q. would be too big to measure.

After we finished our class, we piled back into the cars and were off for dinner at Mac's. Luckily, Megan's mother has nerves of steel. The kind of noise we generate might send a less disciplined driver up the nearest telephone pole.

We all lined up outside the restaurant and made our entrance, one at a time. Heads turned as we filed in. A couple people did classic double takes. Maybe I should have expected the general reaction, but I didn't, so it came as a nice surprise when everyone grinned and nodded or waved at us. Or called out things like "Where are the elephants?" or "Is the circus in town?"

All during dinner, people came by our booths and tables to ask questions. Why were we dressed as clowns? How had we learned to do our makeup? Where had we found our costumes? Emily glowed at the marvelous opportunity to educate an appreciative audience.

Mrs. De Witt had also dressed as a clown, so people asked her a lot of questions, too. She came by our booth later to pass the word that our 4-H group had already been given our first assignment. In a few weeks, we would help in the festivities to open a shopping center.

I felt good all over, just sitting and watching people smile at us. One lady came in looking so cross, it was clear she'd had a rotten day. But the minute she saw us, she began to grin. The grin stayed in place while she waited at the counter for her order, and she was still grinning when she waved at us from the door. As a result, I was entirely unprepared for the final incident of that outing.

A few of us went to the rest room after dinner and everybody had gone back to the cars by the time I came out of the booth, washed my hands, and put on the silk gloves that are part of my outfit.

The door opened, and a lady came in with a little girl about three. "Oh my, Bethie, here's one of the clowns!" The lady chatted for a minute about how cute we looked and what fun we must have "clowning around." Already, I was sick of that phrase. Everybody who said it seemed to think they were the first to think of it. Just as I turned to leave, I felt a vicious pinch. Little Bethie beamed up at me, her tiny fingers reaching for another assault on my thigh.

"Hey!" I said, and hastily dodged.

Bethie's mother smacked her hand. "What made you do a thing like that?" she said, horrified. "What a naughty girl!"

She was still apologizing as I went out the door, suffering more from shock than the injury. I'd always thought everybody loved clowns, especially kids. So how come this little golden-haired cherub had made a direct attack, smiling all the while? I puzzled over that all the way home.

We walked in and caught Mom and Dad eating ice cream with chocolate sauce, and both of them looked really guilty. They've been talking about going on a diet for weeks now.

Dad saw me grinning at him and he patted his stomach. He's got a pot, all right, but only a little one. "We'll start on that diet tomorrow," he said. "So how did they like you at Mac's? Think they'll book you again next weekend?"

"It was okay."

I didn't have to say any more because Emily took over, delivering a full report. "You know what's neat?" she said at last. "Everybody was looking at me, but it wasn't *me* they were seeing at all. It's kind of like I was invisible, hiding inside another person. All they could see was Cricket. It's fun—but it could get really weird after a while."

It was the first time I realized Emily, too, had mixed feelings about the spotlight. I never thought anybody else in the family felt the way I did, welcoming attention but scared of it at the same time.

Both Mom and Dad are friendly, outgoing people. Byron sends everybody a message. You take him the way he is or you don't, and he doesn't much care either way. Emily's more like Mom and Dad except for her nonstop mouth. Maybe that's a way of insisting that people notice her. Well, maybe I do that, too, with my Funny Girl act.

It got too heavy at that point, so I went out to the kitchen for a glass of water. Dad got up and followed me. It startles me sometimes how he picks up on my moods. Mom says it's because he was a middle kid, too, with a brainy older brother and a bratty younger one. He doesn't want me to get lost in the shuffle like he did. I love it when he shows how much he cares about me. It makes up for a lot of lumps and bumps.

"You didn't have much to say, honey," he said, his voice casual. "Anything wrong?"

"Nah. Just didn't feel like battling Emily for equal time." I looked at him and suddenly I blurted the whole story, all about the little kid who'd pinched the nice friendly clown. I couldn't really think of it as a personal attack. But why be mean to a clown?

Dad couldn't figure it out, either. "Kids that age are funny," he said, scratching his chin. "They hear a lot of stories—and they see movies and TV. That means there's a whole lot of fantasy in their lives. Maybe they get mixed up sometimes about what's real and what isn't."

"You mean she didn't know I was real?"

Dad grinned and gestured at my costume. "Well, in that getup, with the wig and the gunk on your face, you don't look like anybody she's apt to meet walking down the street."

He leaned over to kiss my cheek, thought better of it when he saw the white makeup, and settled for a hug.

I went to get out of my costume and makeup and into a long hot shower, feeling better. Even the small bluish bruise on my thigh didn't bring the dark mood back. In my pajamas, I wound a towel

69

around my damp hair and went to the kitchen to get a bedtime snack.

Byron came in from the garage to share my celery slathered with peanut butter, apple slices, and a handful of dates so dry I ended up dunking them in hot chocolate. We stood by the counter in silence except for munching noises.

I suspected he had something on his mind and wasn't sure how to put it in words. As a card-carrying member of the blab-first-and-live-to-regret-it society, I sometimes envy Byron's restraint. When in doubt, he keeps his mouth shut. It's one of those sensible traits that people like me admire but rarely copy.

My brother's routine before he starts to speak is interesting to watch. It's as if the chosen topic has to whir through all the little minicomputers in his brain. Then he clears his throat to alert the listener that the data is ready, and brushes a few locks of hair off his forehead so he can smooth that scarred eyebrow.

That night, all systems go, Byron spoke. "I'm taking Nicole out Friday night after the game."

Then he hesitated so long, I began to wonder if his mental computers had malfunctioned. "Yeah?" I said by way of mild encouragement. "So?"

"So I figure you know her a lot better than I do.

Maybe you could give me a few tips. I mean, you're a girl, too."

Unreal. Not only was it the first time Byron had asked for this kind of advice, he'd never said "you're a girl" in that tone, either. Usually, it sounds like he's saying, "So what can anybody expect?" On his best day, Byron never delivers the phrase with more than a note of mild tolerance, as if he considers my female condition unfortunate, but hardly my fault.

Tonight, he seemed to find it an asset, inasmuch as Nicole shares the affliction. My mind thoroughly boggled, I concentrated for a full thirty seconds on the soggy date I had soaked in my hot chocolate. Somehow I knew I'd better handle my brother's uneasy request with great care.

"You know about her mother? How she let Granny Gus take Nicole to Europe when she was little? And then—she never asked for Nico back again?"

Byron nodded. His mouth tightened.

I said slowly, "Well, that whole area's a little touchy. Not only her relationship with her mother, but—" I told him what Granny Gus had said about wanting to go to the Sunnyside Home, and about Nicole's reaction.

"Poor kid."

"Yeah. But you have to know the background to understand why Nicole's—kind of insecure. There

71

haven't been a lot of people in her life that she could depend on."

"Sounds that way." Byron's voice didn't offer any clues. He stood examining a slice of apple, so I couldn't see his eyes.

"She's sort of shy, too," I said, "for the same reasons." Then the words tumbled out, prodded by strong emotions. "I'm warning you, Byron, and you better listen good. Nicole is one of my very best friends. She's been dumped on by people she should have been able to trust, people who should have cared about her. What I'm saying is, you'd better not hurt her in any way whatsoever or—or—"

I ran out of steam just when I reached the point where I should have cut loose with the heavy ammunition. I figured I'd blown it, anyway, so I ended with the only phrase that came to me, straight out of childhood, at that.

"—or you'll be sorry!"

Incredibly, Byron laughed. Then he totaled me by reaching out to pat my cheek. "If I couldn't fight my own battles," he said, "I bet you'd get out there and fight for me. Wouldn't you, Shell?"

"Of course I would," I said crossly. "You'd do the same for me."

"Are you sure about that?"

"Yeah, matter of fact, I am. In sixth grade, you

threatened to wipe up the sidewalk with old Rotten Rory."

Byron blinked. "Rotten who?"

"Rory Dreyfuss. Remember? He lives down on Halsey. He'd hide behind the hedge in front of his house and throw smushy lemons at us when we were on the way to school. Nicole and Megan and me."

I grinned. "Carly Bennett used to live next door to old Rotten. She said you scared him so bad he nearly wet his pants. And all you did was sort of tower over him while you told him in this very soft voice all the things you were going to do to him if he ever bothered your sister again."

Byron chuckled. "You've got a good memory. Well—any guy picking on three little girls—least I could do—"

I studied my nails. "Nicole thought it was cool."

"Yeah?"

I smiled at him. "She loves movies with a lot of special effects. And pizza—any kind of Italian food—or Mexican or Chinese. She's a champ swimmer and she's getting good at tennis, too. You can talk football, because I bet she knows as much about the game as you do. And—she's really into this clowning thing." I paused. "Does that help?"

For a second, I thought Byron was going to do something terribly embarrassing like hug me. He made one quick move, then caught himself.

"Thanks," he said. "I got a good memory too, Shell. Any time you're wondering about—oh, how guys feel about girls—and why—well, just ask."

I thought about Jon but looked at the clock and shook my head. "I'll take you up on that someday when you can give me a little time. Say, four or five hours." I took the dishes to the sink and rinsed our cups.

Byron said from the door, "Hey, Shell, you don't have to worry about Nicole and me. I think she's—she's something really special."

When I looked up he had gone down the hall. I went to dry my hair and crawl into bed, so tired I ached all over. Still, I couldn't get to sleep for a while. Maybe it was the caffeine in the chocolate. More likely, my brain had gone into overdrive with all the food for thought I'd gathered that day.

On one hand, a downer, the incident with Little Bethie.

But the rest was pure gold:

1. Not all Molly Marines are evil.

2. Math teachers sometimes go to great lengths to conceal marshmallow hearts.

3. Freak-out fact for the day: Big brothers can be *beautiful*.

6

Nicole didn't have much to say on the way home from school that Friday. I saw the tight look around her mouth and suspected she might be talking herself out of the after-game date with Byron.

Megan said abruptly, "Wouldn't you know I'd have to miss the first game?" She saw my startled look. "I told you I have to baby-sit my brothers tonight. Remember?"

"I didn't realize you meant this Friday, game night." My first reaction was rage. Her parents are so insensitive, it's going to be a nightmare when Megan begins to date. I'm sure it never occurs to them to give her priority once in a while when her plans conflict with theirs.

I simmered in silence for a few minutes, then realized that something good might come out of Meg missing the first game. Nicole couldn't very well back out now. She knew my parents wouldn't let me go alone.

"I'll come by for you around six, Nico," I said quickly.

She looked at me. "Your mom won't let you walk home alone." Then she brightened. "You can come with Byron and me afterward."

"Sure, sure. That'd be really cool, going along on your first date. For heaven's sake, it's no biggie. I can find somebody to walk home with."

An hour later, I heard myself singing the same refrain. I'd gone out to practice the routine Mrs. Upjohn had suggested, lobbing the tennis ball against the back of the garage. When Mom got home, she came out to ask what I planned to do after the game.

"You'll be coming home with Megan?"

"Uh—no, she has to baby-sit. Not to worry," I added cheerfully. "I'll find somebody to walk home with."

"Shelley." Her voice had the ominous note that means we'd-better-discuss-this. "Can you be a little more definite? The name of a real live person? Preferably somebody male, six feet tall, and totally responsible?"

I closed my eyes, pained. Mrs. Peggy Lucas, prime contender for Medieval Mother of the Month. Then Jon's voice intervened, and my eyes popped open. He'd been behind the hedge, so he must have heard everything.

"I'm only five ten, Mrs. Lucas, but—do I qualify otherwise? Okay if Shelley walks home with me?"

Mom grinned. "Okay with me if it's okay with her."

She sounded so casual, I felt guilty about bestowing the Medieval Mother medal. "Sure," I said, my mouth dry. "Thanks, Jon. Uh—do you know where we'll be?"

"Yeah, if it's where you usually sit."

He even knew where we always sat at games! I picked up the tennis ball, dropped it, retrieved it, and finally managed a graceless retreat across the deck and into the house.

Mom came in a few minutes later as I sat on the kitchen stool, still stunned. "Jon wanted to know if you could stop for pizza on the way home."

"What did you say? *What did you say?*"

She laughed. "I said okay. That's what I said." She turned from the sink to look at me. "You're to come right home from the pizza place. I want you in by eleven-thirty. Understood?"

"Wow," I breathed. "Yeah. Sure." I recovered enough to hug her. "Is it—could you call this sort of thing—a date?"

Her face looked odd, as if she were trying not to laugh, or maybe she was on the verge of crying. I couldn't decide which.

She reached for her apron on the hook in the broom closet. "Of course it's a date. Isn't that what you're calling it with Nicole and Byron?"

"I guess."

She smiled at me, and her eyes were shinier than usual. Still, I couldn't figure out why she'd be close to tears at a fantastic moment like this.

"You like Jon a lot, don't you?"

"You noticed."

Her laugh sounded a little breathless. "The symptoms were pretty hard to ignore. On both sides, I might add."

I stared at her. "You mean—you think Jon likes *me*?"

"Why do you think he spends so much time out in the yard? Those flower beds would thrive with a third of the attention they get."

I stood hugging myself as if I were trying to hold on to this earth-shaking piece of information, as well as my own magnificent bod. "But—but he didn't ask if he could sit with me at the game—"

My mother sighed. "Give him time. You've been part of a perpetual threesome. You and Nicole and Megan, always together. It's hard for a boy to break into a setup like that. Now Byron's singled out Nicole, and tonight Jon saw his chance to get you alone. Simple as that."

I thought about it for a while. "How come you never told me? I mean, that it might be tough for a guy to ask one of us for a date? Because Megan and Nico and I—we're always together. Why didn't you ever say anything about it before?"

For a minute I wondered whether or not she'd answer. She just stood at the sink, staring out the window, half-peeled potato in one hand and the paring knife in the other. Then she turned and gave me a vague smile.

"It wasn't important," she said, "as long as none of you seemed in any hurry to start dating. I've always thought it's a mistake to push kids into that. Boy-girl parties at an age when they don't even want to be in the same room with each other. Don't you remember the reason you quit the Hike and Bike Club?"

The memory was vivid all right, etched with the anger I'd felt as a ten-year-old. I slammed into the house one afternoon, announcing dramatically that I was through with the club forever. Aware of my

79

parents' feelings about the benefits of this organization, however, I really didn't think they'd let me out.

My mother asked calmly, "What happened?"

"They brought some boys over to square dance," I said crossly. "And that's not the reason I joined."

"No," she agreed, and gave me a long thoughtful look.

"So I quit."

"Will it happen again? Will the boys come back? To square dance?"

"That's what Mrs. Manners said. Is that the most sickening thing you've ever heard?"

"No," my mother said, still maddeningly serene. "But it's right up there on the list."

"Hey, you mean I can quit? You'll let me?"

She shrugged. "Well, you put up a pretty good argument. That isn't the reason you joined the Hike and Bike Club, to square dance—with anybody."

I recalled clearly how pleased I'd been that she understood. I said now, slowly, "I wasn't ready for boys and dancing and dating and stuff, not in fifth grade."

"Of course not," my mother said.

I groaned. "You know something? I still don't feel ready. Jon may end up sorry he offered to walk me home."

Mom gave me another long direct look. "Other people often take you at your own face value, Shelley. Once you convince yourself that you're a—a loser, a lot of people may accept that."

"I don't know what I am," I said flatly. "Mrs. Upjohn was right, I guess. She says I'm still on the assembly line and I shouldn't be impatient. But how can you be patient when you know you're nothing but a—an unformed blob?"

"Mrs. Upjohn? Your P.E. teacher? Isn't she the one you call a—"

"A Molly Marine, yeah. But I was wrong. She's really neat."

My mother looked startled. "What else did she say?"

I suffered a sudden attack of shyness, so I busied myself washing my hands, then rummaging in the drawer for the silver to set the table.

Aware of my mother's gaze, I mumbled, "Oh, she thinks I have—potential."

"Enormous potential."

"She said limitless," I blurted. Then I nearly lost the last remnants of poise when my mother grabbed me and hugged me. "Watch it," I said weakly. "You almost got stabbed by a fistful of forks."

I felt good about that talk, really close to her. My parents think we're all terrific, and we realize they're prejudiced. It helps a lot, though, especially when everything in your life is a shambles, to know somebody's in your corner.

That evening, I took so long changing my clothes to put together a sensational outfit (a pale green sweater and jeans to reflect the school colors) that I didn't have much time for dinner.

As usual, Emily yammered through the meal. Then she fixed me with her glorious eyes and asked a blunt question. "You gonna let Jon kiss you on the first date?"

I choked on my soup and glared at her, blinking my watering eyes fast so I wouldn't smear my eye makeup.

Dad said firmly, "That'll be enough, Emily." Then he looked at her, curious. "Did you honestly think she'd answer a question like that?"

Emily gave him a silly grin and shook her head. "Then why'd you ask?"

"Well, there's always a *chance*," she said, annoyed. "If I catch her off guard or something. How am I ever going to find out the really interesting stuff if somebody doesn't tell me?"

My mother suffered a coughing spell over that one. At last she murmured, "You've got time, honey. Lots and lots of time."

For once, however, Emily had a point. I thought

about her plaintive question all the way down to Nicole's corner. Lately, Byron and I had achieved a peaceful plateau in our relationship, something I never dreamed would happen. So maybe Emily hoped I'd turn into a helpful role-model Big Sister some day, one who'd answer all her nutty, nosy questions. Just thinking about the one she'd asked, I felt my stomach flip.

Relieved, I saw Nicole running to meet me. The last thing I wanted to consider right now was the far-out, remote, utterly terrifying possibility that Jon might kiss me tonight.

Our Mesa Marauders played the Tremont Trojans that evening. It was a squeaker, 28–27, our favor. I felt happy about that, of course, but something that had nothing to do with school spirit pleased me even more. Byron, Mesa's tight-end hero, would be great company for Nicole afterward. They could replay all his triumphs on the field.

Jon came to sit behind us during the last quarter, leaning over to comment on every play, so I had a real problem following the action. We stayed until the stadium cleared, then walked to the gate where Byron had told Nicole he'd meet her and waited till he appeared, fifteen minutes later.

Byron wore a broad grin, naturally. After that game, he was entitled. It surprised me a little to feel so much fierce pride in my brother. He looked absolutely smashing in a suede jacket and Levi's, his hair still damp from the shower.

"Great game," Jon told him. "What a cliff-hanger!"

Nicole just stood smiling at him, looking shy but happy. She'd never been more beautiful. Byron's gaze remained on her face all the time he was talking to Jon and me.

We finally said good-bye, and as Jon and I walked toward the pizza place, I stopped thinking about my brother and my best friend. It took all my energy to concentrate on Jon and me.

Luckily, right from the first, we found a lot to talk about, the game and how we felt about high school and the classes we shared. Soon I relaxed and actually enjoyed myself, though I could never remember afterward what kind of pizza we ate or if I had a Coke or Seven-Up.

It turned out we liked a lot of the same things, though I'm crazy about Linda Ronstadt and she doesn't even make his list. Same with Kenny Rogers. Jon thinks he's fantastic, but I'm not as impressed.

It was fun, finding out how we felt about music and movies and books. And food. While we were on that subject, I told him about Emily and her experimental sandwiches.

"You're kidding!" he said, and laughed. "Cu-

cumbers and salami? She must have a strong stomach."

At that point, a crowd of kids from school came in, still talking about our victory over Tremont. I saw Foxie bringing up the rear, but too late to turn my face or hide behind my napkin.

"Well, hiiii, Shelley." Then she turned to give Jon a full-voltage smile. "Hi, Jon. Were you both at the game?"

Jon grinned. "Wouldn't have missed it."

Foxie discussed the winning touchdown for a few minutes, giving me a great view of her back. In her expensive sweater and Calvin Kleins, I had to admit it was just that—a great view.

Then she turned to me with the small smile that meant she'd come up with a line intended to draw blood. "Didn't recognize you for a minute, Shell. Out of your clown costume, I mean. You're sure a natural, you know that? I mean, anybody with hairy knees—"

"Sure, and it helps to have a nose that lights up—without batteries." Horrified, I realized I'd responded as predictably as those dogs in the famous Russian experiments. Ring a bell, and Shelley springs into action. Make a rotten crack, and she's the kid who can top it. Especially when it's dump-on-Shelley time.

85

Somebody yelled at Foxie, and she sauntered down the aisle.

A dark silence descended. I played with my napkin, tearing off small pieces and rolling them into little balls.

"Hey," Jon said after a moment, forcing me to look at him. "Why do you let her do that?"

"What?"

"Stick a knife between your ribs." His green eyes flashed with anger. "You even help."

"Do I?"

"Yeah, you do." He reached for my hand. "She's mean, Shelley. And she knows she's mean. She likes it. Did you see the way she looked when she made that crack about hairy knees?"

I released the breath I'd been holding. "Yeah, well—maybe you're right. I've been wondering myself why—"

"Why what?"

I swallowed hard, in so deep now I couldn't retreat. "—why I let her do it."

Another silence. Jon seemed to realize he was still holding my hand. He dropped it, then touched it again gently before he picked up his glass of water.

It was the first time all evening that I'd seen him act uneasy or nervous. I wished desperately that I knew what was going on inside his head.

86

"I guess we better go," he said. "Your Mom—"

"Yeah, I guess we better."

On the short walk home, he picked up the conversation where Foxie had interrupted it, asking about Emily's more memorable sandwiches. I couldn't be sure if he really wanted to know, or if he'd just grasped at the first subject that might rescue us from another heavy silence.

He took me to my door and waited till I'd unlocked it. Then he backed down one step and nodded as I thanked him. "Shelley?"

"Yeah?"

"Promise me something?"

"Uh—what?"

"Promise me you won't let Foxie zing you any more."

I tried to laugh, but it sounded phony, I almost winced. "How am I going to do that?"

"I'd say, belt her right in the mouth, but"—he made a low sound, close to a chuckle—"she's a lot bigger than you. So why don't you use all that talent you have for bright remarks—and hit back?"

I lost my voice for several seconds. When I finally recovered, it came out a little hoarse, not like my normal voice at all. "Okay, I'll try."

Jon nodded again and loped down the sidewalk, whistling.

I went inside, completely confused. He hadn't tried to kiss me. I couldn't answer Emily's question even if I'd wanted to.

If it hadn't been for the way I acted with Foxie, *would* Jon have kissed me? I couldn't answer that one, either.

7

Nicole and I were on the phone the next afternoon for more than an hour. My Mom clocks my calls as a rule, especially when they run over half an hour. She'll stick her head in my room and point to her watch, a not-so-subtle signal for me to wind up the conversation.

That Saturday afternoon she let us talk. Maybe she figured I'd earned a reward for scrubbing floors and washing windows like a madwoman all morning. It hadn't diverted my mind from the questions about last night, but apparently I'd won a few Brownie points. Maybe Mom remembers how much it used to mean to her to compare notes with a friend when she first started dating. Hard to say. One neat thing about my mother, she seems to recall a lot about her growing-up years. She understands better than a lot of parents do when Byron or Emily or I have a problem.

Nicole certainly hadn't encountered any difficulty with her first date. She rattled on for several minutes. Byron had talked about everything that interested her: football, special-effects movies, clowning. They'd gone for Chinese food after they left Jon and me. Byron told her he liked Italian and Mexican food, too. And they had a date to play tennis Sunday afternoon.

"You know, Shell," she said, "he was so nice, I didn't feel shy at all."

I laughed to myself, pleased that Byron had used all the stuff I gave him during that briefing. Good for him.

Nicole is sensitive about other people, even if she doesn't have Megan's special ability to heal the sore spots she detects. Right away, she picked up on my evasive replies to questions about Jon and me.

"Shell? Come on, what happened? He didn't try to—uh—um—he didn't—did he?"

"No," I said. "Jon? Of course not." I sounded as bleak as I felt. The only thing worse than having a whole lot more happen on a first date than I'd expected or wanted was—having nothing happen at all.

"Might as well tell you," I said at last. "I came off like a real nerd."

I heard her quick intake of breath, but she didn't say anything, waiting for me to spell it out. I told her about the disastrous exchange with Foxie, not sparing myself. In a way, it was a relief to tell Nicole that I was aware of this routine that Foxie and I had going. The thing was, Jon didn't understand it any better than I did, and he'd made it clear he didn't like it.

"Oh, Shell," Nicole said when I finished, "Jon's right, you know. That Foxie is so *mean*. And Gran says girls like that usually pick on people who don't fight back. Maybe if you—"

"That's what Jon said, for me to hit back. I—I just don't know if I can," I said miserably. "Joking around with people is one thing. But, Nico, if I think I've hurt somebody, I—I end up hurting worse than they do."

"I know."

A brief uneasy silence.

"Well," she said, "maybe you'll get a brilliant idea how to handle it. Foxie's trying to hurt *you*, you know. So the next time she rips you, don't hesitate to rip her right back."

"Sure."

"The only reason Jon reacted like that is because he likes you."

"Sure."

"He does," she insisted. "I saw the way he looked at you last night."

"That was before he saw what happened with Foxie." I swallowed past the lump in my throat. "I swear, every time she gets her knife out, I grab it and self-destruct."

We kicked it around for a while longer, then changed the subject before we got any more depressed. Megan's birthday would be coming up soon, and Nicole said Granny Gus and Tilly wanted to give a surprise party for her. So we ended the conversation on that happy note.

Late that afternoon, I went out to bounce the ball again, hoping that Jon might appear but not really expecting that he would. Ten minutes after I began my practice session, I heard him call to me from the hedge.

"Have you got some kind of deal with the people who make those things? Shelley Lucas, tennis-ball tester?"

I was so delighted to see him, I never even thought about giving him a simple explanation. No, I went barreling down the same road I always took, the let's-laugh-it-up-about-Lucas trip.

"My P.E. teacher says this is good for klutzy people. I can walk clear across the living room now without tripping over the pattern in the carpet, so—" I saw something flicker in his eyes and felt my face burn. In that horrible moment, tears threatened for the second time that day.

"Mrs. Upjohn says—she thinks the exercises might help—you know—to develop eye-hand coordination." I didn't look at him.

"Good!" Jon said with unnecessary emphasis. He seemed to realize that, because he laughed. "I have a few problems along that line, too. It's one reason I don't care much about contact sports. Well, I'm not crazy about pain and agony, either. Seems to me, if it's a sport, there should be some fun involved."

I grinned at him, grateful that he'd given me a few seconds to pull myself together.

"Hey, if you've got another racket, why don't we use the hedge as a net, give us both a workout?"

It turned out to be a terrific idea. An hour later, I went inside to shower, exhausted and weak from laughing. We'd only kept track of missed balls, which racked up points in the other player's favor. The final score was hysterical, Jon leading by something like 67–12. Still, he claimed I'd improved in just that one session. We'd have to do it again, he said, maybe tomorrow.

I went to sleep that night marveling at the way life bounced me up and down like the tennis ball we'd used that day. I'd better develop the same resiliency, I thought wearily.

The highlight of the following Tuesday was the event I'd anticipated since the clown classes began. A professional clown came for a visit to share a few tricks of his trade.

Blinko turned out to be a skinny little guy with wispy gray hair. His wizened face looked comical even before he put on his makeup. "Ha!" he exclaimed as he made his entrance into Mrs. De Witt's crowded family room. "Dozens of beautiful clowns-in-training, and all of them on the floor—at my feet! You'll inspire me to do my best work." He went up the aisle we'd left for him, grasping hands and blowing kisses.

But the minute he sat in the chair before the low table Mrs. De Witt had placed at the end of the room, he dropped the hammy routine and settled down to business.

First, he went through the makeup, step by step, his tramp face emerging—a big white mouth, white around the eyes, red on cheeks and forehead and nose, the beard applied with a stipple brush. Along the way, he threw out tips about keeping our makeup in a cool place, bracing our arms when we did the lines on our clown faces, and blending the red with a tissue.

He'd brought a couple of his costumes along, funny hats that perched on his bushy gray wig, baggy pants and coats with signs on them: BLINKO THE GREAT, WIZARD FOR HIRE, THE WORLD'S FIRST CAMPY CLOWN.

Then he beckoned to Megan. "Come on, honey, let's show the folks how to walk and skip and act like a *clown*. What's your name? Megan? Oh, I like that." As she joined him, flushed and self-conscious, he held out a white scarf. "Present for a pretty girl. Oh, you'd rather have a colored one?" A rapid movement with his agile hands, and he held a red scarf.

He peered at her smiling face, ignoring the scatter of applause. "Red's not your favorite color? Well, how about"—another quick gesture—"blue?" And again the scarf seemed to change color, magically.

There were a lot of props hidden in the enormous pockets of his costumes, a wand that turned into a bouquet of flowers, then back into a wand that sprinkled confetti. After a few minutes, Blinko produced a feather duster and showed us how to put together a skit, using Megan as his partner. She pretended to be allergic to the feathers, sneezing loudly when the duster came close to her.

By the time Blinko went through the exaggerated movements of a clown, skipping and jumping around the space we cleared, Megan was working with him like a pro. Nicole nudged me as we watched the two little people hop around, pretending to chase each other, beaming as the audience clapped and laughed.

"Megan's almost as good as he is," Nicole said softly under all the noise.

I nodded. It pleased me even more to see how much she was enjoying herself. She didn't look like a mouse anymore.

When Blinko turned to the box of balloons, Megan came back to sit with us, her face radiant. "Did it look okay?" she asked.

"Terrific. You were fantastic," we assured her. I hid my grin as she nodded and settled back. Her question had been automatic. She knew she'd done a good job.

Blinko rapped for attention. Then he asked Emily and Foxie to help distribute the balloons, some of them long and thin, others short and fat. To me, the demonstration that followed was fascinating. Small red balloons turned into rosy apples. Others were transformed into a variety of animals, long low-slung dachshunds and perky poodles, complete with puffs on the ends of their tails. Blinko even fashioned a pink swan out of two skinny balloons.

As I suspected, my main difficulty came with the initial step, blowing up those long thin balloons. Mrs. De Witt went from group to group telling us not to puff our cheeks out, but to blow from the diaphragm.

I had very little success, but I giggled when I glanced across the room at my sister. Emily was already on her third balloon, looking more expert by the minute. Naturally. With her inexhaustible supply of hot air, how could she miss?

For me, that hour passed much too quickly. Everyone crowded around Blinko at the end, so I didn't have a chance to talk to him. But I heard what he said to Megan, after he thanked her for being his partner.

"I think it's real great that you want to work with kids, honey. And you'll find out something kinda interesting. Those sick kids give you more than you give to them. Every time. Just remember one thing. Never use a pump to blow up balloons when you visit little ones in the hospital. Scares them to death. Those pumps look too much like the needles that hurt them."

Standing on tiptoe, I could see his silly green hat bobbing as he talked.

"Another thing to watch out for—" He laughed. "Some of those little guys may come up after they've watched you for a while, and they'll give you a kick in the shins. Or else they'll hit you. Or maybe pinch you wherever they can reach a place for a good ole nip."

I drew in my breath, thinking of Little Bethie at Mac's last week.

"First time it happens," Blinko said, "you just plain can't understand it. Makes you feel real bad. So I'd like to explain what I think goes on in those little heads.

"You gotta realize they're entirely tuned in to what you're doing and what they think you are. It's make-believe. It isn't real to them. They don't know there's a *person* under the crazy clothes and makeup. Doesn't look like anything they ever saw up close before. So one thing they're doing is testing, I guess."

Megan murmured something I didn't catch.

"You sure do," Blinko told her firmly. "You bend down and you tell that little sucker, 'Hey, there's a *person* inside this funny-looking outfit. So don't hurt me. I cry like anybody else. I just came to have a good time with you, to make you laugh.' That usually works. If I was you, I'd take it as a compliment. When it happens like that, it means you did a good job. All those little folks could see was—fantasy. Magic."

I drifted toward the door, thinking so hard I bumped into Foxie as she tried to edge past me.

She snapped her fingers in front of my face. "You

don't look like you're tracking, A.D. That doesn't just stand for Acey Deucey, you know. How about Absolutely Dingy? Suits you better."

I stared at her, jolted so abruptly from Blinko's nice raspy voice to her slow drawl that I didn't stop to think before I spoke. That gave me a crumb of comfort later. For once, I didn't respond to her needling with my usual deft maneuver, catching the pie in midair and throwing it in my own face.

"Foxie," I said, "go play somewhere else, will you? Maybe in the middle lane on Highway 805." No, it wasn't a great line, but a lot better than the ones I usually came up with.

Her eyes widened, icy for a moment. Then they narrowed as she gave an uncertain spurt of laughter. "Wow. Where's A.D.'s famous sense of humor?" She went through the door before she turned for another shot. "I know! You're ticked off because I made that crack in front of Jon the night of the game. Is that it?"

I felt myself begin to shake with anger. But before I could say a word, I heard Emily's clear voice behind me.

"If I were you, Big Mama, I'd think twice about making fun of anybody's initials."

Foxie's eyes spit blue sparks. "If it isn't Cricket, the All-American Mouth. Does your sister need you to defend her?"

"Emily," I said, and put my hand on her arm. Startled, I felt her trembling, too.

But she was off and running. "She doesn't need anybody to defend her against you, Lorraine *Gwendolyn* Foxworth."

Gwendolyn? I saw Foxie wince. She never made a secret of the way she felt about a perfectly good name like Lorraine. I had a hunch she hated her middle name even more. How on earth had Emily found out what it was?

"I'll fix you," Foxie said between her teeth. "Both of you. See if I don't." She glanced at me, her face scarlet and twisted with anger. "Next time you're out with Jon, you'd better look around for me." She ran toward her mother's car easing to the curb in front.

Emily wailed softly, "Oh, I'm sorry, Shell. I shot my mouth off, all right. And it just made it worse for you. I didn't mean—"

"Don't you dare say you didn't mean it." My laugh was a little shaky. "You were wonderful!"

"I was?"

"You sure were." I steered her toward Mrs. Malloncrodt's car. "We'll talk about it when we get home. And I'll pin a few medals on you here and there."

"But—but the next time you see Foxie, she'll slice you up like—like pastrami."

"No," I said with more confidence than I felt.

"All I have to do is call her Gwendolyn, and she'll back off. How'd you find out her middle name?"

Emily smiled. "Oh, I know someone who lives next to somebody who went to Lincoln. That's where Foxie went to junior high. This girl said at graduation, a couple people laughed out loud when they read off Foxie's name on her diploma. Boys may like her, but girls don't."

"You got that right. And you got me off the hook, babe. I owe you one."

At home, we talked for a long time while I fixed macaroni and cheese for dinner and a big salad. Emily set the table and never once commented that it was her night for kitchen duty. If she'd thanked me, it would have embarrassed both of us.

I could hardly believe it, Emily defending me against the meanest mouth in Mesa. My insides turned to jelly, just thinking about the inevitable confrontation when Foxie would do a number on me right in front of Jon. I knew she'd follow through on her threat.

Still, in those moments in the kitchen, I didn't worry too much about how I'd handle her. The thing that really upset me was what Foxie was planning in that devious mind of hers to get back at my sister.

8

That Friday afternoon, Jon and I batted the tennis ball back and forth across the hedge for almost an hour. I tried to concentrate on the game, but my attention kept straying, admiring the way the sun struck coppery sparks from his hair.

Abruptly, he blurted out an invitation to the movies. "Hey, Shell, you wanta go see *Born in Space* tomorrow night? Will your parents let you go to the seven o'clock show? If I get you home by eleven-thirty like last time?"

It would be perfect, because the movie was showing at a theater nearby. We could walk there and back. I knew my parents wouldn't be thrilled about the idea of a car date until they were sure the guy was a squared-away driver. Only one problem. Megan's surprise party had been scheduled for Saturday night.

"Oh, Jon, I can't."

He looked away, flipping the ball in the air and catching it. "Okay. Just thought I'd ask."

I said hastily, "I've been dying to see that movie. But—but Nicole's giving a birthday party for Megan tomorrow night. A surprise. I just—I just can't cancel out on something like that."

"Oh." His face relaxed. "Well—how about next weekend?"

"Great. I think next Saturday would be okay. I'll ask."

Jon nodded, hit the ball to me, and flubbed my return. Maybe it rattled him, asking me to go out, though I found that hard to believe. More likely, he'd missed the ball on purpose, trying to boost my confidence. These practice sessions had helped a lot. I wasn't close to beating him, but the scores weren't quite as humiliating now.

In a way I felt pleased that the movie date had been postponed. I'd have a whole week to think about it, plan what I'd wear, rehearse possible dialogue. I always feel a little cheated when something terrific happens to me without warning. I don't have a chance to enjoy looking forward to it.

That weekend whizzed by. The best part was Megan's party, of course. Ten of her friends were hidden around the dimly lighted living room of the condo when the doorbell rang. Nicole warned us to be quiet as she went to admit Megan.

We could hear her in the entry hall. "Nico, I still think it'd be better if we waited till Shelley can practice with us. But I called earlier. She's gone somewhere."

Nicole said casually, "She said Jon asked her to go see *Born in Space*. Why don't we work out in here? I thought we'd have more room." She came down the two steps into the living room, my signal to replace the plug of the big corner lamp.

In the brighter light, I peeked around the end of the couch to catch Megan's bewildered expression as she saw gaily wrapped gifts piled on the coffee table. Then we all rushed out of our hiding places yelling "Surprise! Happy birthday!"

The great thing is, we really surprised her. She hadn't picked up on the abruptly terminated conversations at school that week, discussions that cut off when she walked up to somebody in the corridor or came into a classroom. At least two of the girls had slipped and mentioned "the party Saturday night" in front of her, but she hadn't caught those clues, either.

"Wow," she kept saying, flushed and smiling. "This

is so nice of you. Look at those beautiful packages. All for me?"

"The cards say 'For Megan.' You got any I.D.?" Then I had to laugh and hug her. She's always overwhelmed when somebody does something nice for her. Little Orphan Megan. She never seems to realize that everybody loves her the minute they find out what a neat person she is.

A strange mood came over me that night. I'd space in and out, so some of the time I seemed to be outside the action, observing and making mental notes. Sure, I had fun with the rest of them. At the same time, part of me stood aside and tried to figure out what was happening to Nicole and Megan and me—and the other girls at that birthday party.

It struck me first when we sat on the floor around the couch, watching Megan open her presents. Half of us had given her the sort of thing we'd like as gifts, pretty scarves and jewelry and fancy cosmetic kits, the kind that have different shades of eye shadow and creme and blusher, lots of stuff to experiment with.

The rest of the girls came with the same presents they'd given her when she was ten or twelve. Stuffed animals, cutesy stationery with little mice or bunny rabbits on every page, and the figurines we used to love in grade school, everything from Holly Hobby to Miss Piggy. Little-girl things.

Megan might be little, I mused, but she wasn't *a little girl* anymore, even though she was younger than the rest of us. Did the girls who gave her floppy-eared dogs and cunning stationery think of her that way? As a kid who still loved everything with a kitten or puppy motif?

I glanced around the group, laughing and talking as Tilly and Nicole served snacks and soft drinks. It dawned on me then that the ones who had selected kiddy presents were still in the little-girl category themselves. Like Megan (and Nicole and me until a few short weeks ago) they never dated. They went around in groups of three or four or five, giggling a lot over private jokes. They even reverted to grade-school behavior sometimes, shooting rubber bands in the classroom, even staging food fights at the lunch table.

I stopped making notes at that point, really upset by the questions prickling in my mind. Was it just that we were growing up? I'd always thought about maturity as a kind of mystical thing that happened eventually once you'd made the long gradual climb through days and months and years. To me, the key word had been "gradual." That evening it rocked me a little, as I wondered if some of us had crossed that invisible line so quickly *we didn't even realize it yet.*

Nicole didn't count. She was older, almost sixteen. But what had happened to the rest of us? We'd undergone a strange, subtle change. I could see the signs as I studied the group, hear it in the widely varying topics in the feverish hopscotch conversation. But most of the differences were in things I sensed, rather than saw or heard.

Even at the time, I felt torn, almost like two people. One me was happy because I knew I'd changed. I'd wanted to change, hadn't I? To grow up? Another me felt sad, aching with the knowledge that I'd lost something forever.

I looked at Susie Knight, pillow-fight champ at a dozen different slumber parties. And at Rhonda Cleary, who'd established another record at those midnight gatherings, one that had never been equaled—a rolling burp that lasted for a full ten seconds.

Crazy. Because I didn't feel like laughing at those memories. Right in the middle of Megan's sensational birthday party, I almost bawled.

By Monday morning, with the prospect of seeing Jon in two classes, only six days remaining till our movie date, the sun shone on me again. The only puzzling thing was why the blue vapors had lasted so long. And, perhaps, why I seemed to be the only one in my crowd suffering these bizarre growing pains.

During the weekend, my parents went into consultation about my date with Jon, but I wasn't sure why. They liked him a lot, and the movie was PG rated. Were they arguing about my curfew? I'll never know for sure.

In the master bedroom, behind a closed door, their voices rose and fell for nearly half an hour on Sunday afternoon. My only clue came from a few words that I caught, and not exactly by chance. I have to admit I had the door to my room open, trying my best to overhear that discussion.

All I got was one line from my mother, a little muffled so I only caught the words, not what she meant by them. "For heaven's sake, she's only fifteen years old—"

They told me later that they figured eleven-thirty would be a reasonable check-in hour after a three-hour movie. Otherwise, I'd have to be in by eleven.

"We're only talking about Friday and Saturday nights," my mother said firmly. "Not Sunday and never on school nights. Okay?"

"Gotcha. Thanks, Mom." I added, relieved, "I was pretty sure you'd come through with the same curfew you gave Byron at first, but—but I didn't know about Daddy. . . ." My voice trailed off, giving her an opening in case she cared to fill me in on Dad's views.

She didn't. Her smile wasn't even the kind you could call cryptic. (That's one of those words that throw you a curve. It doesn't mean "eerie" or "weird," but "secret" or "obscure." I hate it when words don't mean what they should from the sound of them.) In this case, Mom's smile said it all: *That's all you're going to get out of me.*

I was happy to settle for that, thinking about the wonderful weekend coming up, a movie with Jon on Saturday night and our clowning debut at the new shopping center on Sunday.

I hit the books like a dedicated drone all Sunday afternoon and every evening but one. On Tuesday after school, Megan and I got into our clown costumes and went over to Nicole's to rehearse.

Granny Gus and Tilly giggled over us as if they were a couple of kids our age.

"I was born sixty-five years too soon, and that's a fact." Granny sat on the couch, her tiny feet barely touching the floor. She gave a little bounce. "Never had anything when I was a girl that was half as much fun as this clowning business. My heavenly days, Nicole! If you don't look a fright with that beard!"

Tilly came from the kitchen, wiping her hands on her apron. "You girls have done a real fine job. Working so hard on your costumes—and learning how to make up your faces—"

Nicole froze, her hands deep in the pockets of her baggy jacket. "You better pray hard we don't *fall* on our faces—when it isn't even part of the act. I—am—so—scared. What if I trip over these big old dumb shoes?" She looked down at the clunky workboots painted red to match her plaid pants. Then she peered at us. Even with the white stuff around her eyes, we could see the alarmed expression in them.

"You'll be great," Megan said firmly.

I patted my rear. "I'm the one doing the pratfalls, remember? If anybody should be worrying, it's me. I'm black and blue back there already. You ever stop to think how you wear *that* in a sling?"

Granny and Tilly chuckled, but Nicole just blew out her breath in a big sigh.

"Besides," Megan said hastily, "we're in disguise. You know? That's the good thing about being clowns. If something goes wrong, who's gonna know it isn't part of the act? Even if they do, they won't know who we are."

"I'll know," Nicole muttered. "Granny, do we have to knock off at nine? I need so much practice. Oh, I'll never be ready by Sunday. And there'll be seventy million people at that shopping center."

"Don't go borrowing trouble, love," Granny said serenely. "You'll all be ready, see if you aren't. Tilly and I'll get out of your way now. You'll have two hours before dinner and two hours afterward. Plenty of time."

They disappeared down the hall, and we went to work.

"Want me to go first? I got to practice with Blinko, so I know what I want to do." Megan's tiny mouth looked so funny within the huge red lips drawn around it that Nicole and I just nodded and then grinned at each other.

I don't think either of us suspected how good she'd be, even though we'd seen her with Blinko. We sat, fascinated, on the couch as Megan in slow motion and with broad gestures went through her skit. I found myself leaning forward as I followed the pantomime.

Walking, walking. A sudden stop. Afraid. Of what? A dog? Yes. Now she scolded herself. Mustn't be a coward. She approached the dog. A very *small* dog. She drew back, then reached for it again, timidly. Petted it. Stopped to go through all her pockets. Ah, a tidbit. She reached forward. Panic again, withdrawing. At last—slowly, slowly—she fed the dog. Smiled happily. Stroked the dog. She ended sitting crosslegged, cuddling the little dog against her cheek.

Nicole and I sighed, then looked at each other startled as we realized we'd both been holding our breath. We applauded wildly.

"Oh, Meg, I could see that dog!" I exclaimed. "It's one of those funny long-hairs. You know, like little mops with black beady eyes."

"No, it's a poodle. A tiny one, a teacup." Nicole laughed. "Megan, you rat, you're a natural. Blinko gives you a few tips and you rehearse once and you're perfect. It's not *fair*."

Megan insisted she wasn't that good, but she sounded pleased. Nicole had been right, I thought. Megan was a fast study, yes, and a born mime on top of that. But the best part was—she knew it!

A few minutes later, Nicole said she'd better perform next before she lost her nerve. Megan and I watched, puzzled, as she went across the living room and up the two steps to the tiled entry hall. She turned to face us. Then she began to dance in those enormous cloddy workboots, the clumsiest, most ridiculous soft shoe I'd ever seen.

Megan and I howled—until Nicole stopped to ask crossly if we were laughing at *her* because she looked like an idiot. Or was the dance really funny?

"It's hilarious," I moaned, dabbing at my eyes.

"It's killingly funny," Megan agreed.

Nicole looked at us both for a long moment. Finally she nodded. "Okay. Granny and Tilly think so, too, but I knew you guys would be honest. But listen, I've gotta have something else. These shoes weigh a ton. A couple minutes dancing, that's all I can take."

We discussed a few possibilities.

Megan finally came up with a winner. "You're

shy, Nick. I mean, you're naturally shy. So why don't you use that? You could work up a whole routine, hiding behind another clown, holding your hands up over your face. Hey, that'd be good. It would show off the slogan buttons pinned on your gloves."

It worked. By the time Granny called us to dinner, even Nicole felt she'd be ready by Sunday.

All I needed was more practice in falling. Most of my act was simple, handing out my "cards," the corny riddles and jokes I'd collected.

Between homework and practicing pratfalls, both my fanny and my brain were battered by Saturday night, ready for recess. Unfortunately, the movie barely rated a 6 on my scale, too much talk from the scientists to suit me. And none of them acted scared out of their skulls as they certainly should have been about the awful lizard creatures that came from outer space.

Jon generously gave the show an 8 because of the special effects. Afterward, over pizza, he agreed that all the talking had been a drag. Brushing a lock of red hair off his forehead, he grinned at me, his eyes emerald green in the bright overhead light.

"How'd you feel about them calling the lady scientist Bunny?"

I groaned. "Not enough time to cover that subject. Only an hour left before I turn into a pumpkin. But you can bet the writer was a macho moron.

113

Thought it was funny, probably. Lady scientist, brains enough for any three guys. In real life, you call somebody like that Bunny, and you get a free facelift."

Jon laughed. "Shelley's a neat name, you know that?"

"Thanks. I guess I lucked out. With Mom doing a number on poets—do you realize the guy's name was Percy Bysshe Shelley? And poor Byron—he had to fight half the kids at school over his name. But what if Mom had seriously considered Ezra Pound?"

Jon grinned. "My Dad named me."

"I think Jon's a really nice name."

He looked at me in a way that made my heart wham against my ribs.

"Wish I had my driver's license." He sighed. "Two more months. Mom says I can use her car then. We could go to the beach, movies across town, maybe even up in the mountains." He must have seen me stir uneasily. "Wouldn't you like that? We could go anywhere you say."

"It isn't that I wouldn't like those places. They sound neat, but—" I squirmed. How do you tell a guy your parents won't let you go on a car date until they check out his driving skills? "Thing is, my Mom and Dad— Well, it's Byron's fault, actually. When he first started to drive, he went through a dumb

114

phase. Showing off, heavy foot on the gas. He'd be grounded and—minute he got behind the wheel again, he'd burn rubber before he got out of the driveway."

Jon watched me, no expression on his face.

I went on, sounding a little desperate. If I couldn't be totally honest with him, it might be better to find that out right now. I crossed my fingers, praying he'd understand.

"So—one day he totaled the car. Lucky, though. He got out of it with a broken collarbone and a cut over his eyebrow. The next day Dad took him out in the garage and—the conversation almost peeled the paint off the walls." I laughed, remembering how Mom had sent Emily to her room when she'd caught her in the kitchen listening.

"Byron came in looking a little scorched around the edges, and he didn't have wheels for a long long time. Must have done some good, though. His girls say he's a wonderful driver." I added forcefully, "He better be. He'll have Nicole with him now."

A short, tense silence.

Jon cleared his throat. "What are you saying? That I'll have to—to prove myself to your Dad? Before he'll let you ride with me?"

I felt tears burning behind my eyes. Staring at my plate, I nodded unhappily.

"Mmm. If you were me, would you stand still for something like that?"

I hesitated, still not looking at him. But I'd heard a wry amusement in his voice. So I nodded again.

"Why?"

I looked up and went for broke. "Because I'm worth it," I said softly.

Jon gave a shout of laughter. "Damn straight! Never thought I'd hear you say it, though. Right on target. That's my girl." He leaned forward. "You are my girl, aren't you, Shell?"

I couldn't have said a word right then even if somebody had offered me eighty million dollars. So I nodded for the third time.

"Let's get out of here," he said.

About three minutes later, I realized I'd been hearing one silly phrase in my head, over and over. *Ready or not, ready or not, ready or not . . .*

Midway along the first block, an equal distance between streetlights, Jon paused, took my face between his hands, lifted it, and kissed me.

"Mmm," he said.

"Mmm-hmm," I said. I'd been ready.

There are six blocks between the pizza place and my house. Jon kissed me six times on the way home. But he merely touched my cheek when he said good night at the front door.

I knew then that he'd been shy and uncertain,

116

too. And he certainly hadn't wanted Byron or either of my parents to see him kissing me. Maybe that was the reason he hadn't made a move the night we came home from the game.

He wanted me to be his girl. He liked my name. He liked *me*.

I tiptoed down the hall past Emily's bedroom. Wait till she heard about my second date. Well— I'd tell her about some of it, anyway.

9

During September and October in southern California, we sometimes suffer from something the weathermen call "a Santa Ana condition"—hot dry winds from the desert that suck the moisture out of your skin until it feels tight and stretchy and horrid. The sound of wind makes me nervous and irritable. Pretty soon the roots of my hair begin to itch, and my teeth ache. I always feel better when the fall rains come and the weather turns cooler.

That night I was vaguely aware of the rising wind each time I woke to turn over in bed. Sure enough, Sunday dawned with a sun that turned mean and brassy by nine o'clock. Looking out of the window over the sink, I muttered under my breath. It would not be a pure joy wearing a lot of makeup and our clown costumes on a day hot enough to singe the feathers off a duck.

Emily lingered after breakfast to help me clean up the kitchen, fascinated by the things I chose to share with her about last night. Then, true to form, she zeroed in with questions about details I'd withheld.

"So—did he kiss you?"

I looked at her and laughed. If she'd been a puppy, she would have been panting, tail swishing, long pink tongue lolling. "Come on, Emily, what do you think?"

She flushed. "Yeah, I guess that was kind of—personal." Two beats. "But did he?"

"Yes," I said formally.

She sighed.

I could almost hear the wheels spinning in her head. She might as well push her luck and ask some more questions. What did she have to lose?

"I wish you'd tell me, Shell. You never have—and I can't help wondering. Was that the first time?"

"The first time I ever kissed anybody? Hardly." But, as usual, I blew the attempt at sounding worldly when I giggled. I couldn't help it when I recalled all three of the guys Emily seemed so curious about.

Maybe the first one shouldn't even count. That

was Donny Anderson in fourth grade, and I knew somebody must have dared him to do it. As I was walking home from the store one day, he jumped out at me from behind a tree and kissed me. Afterward, I wondered if he regretted accepting the dare, because I pasted him a good one before I ran home.

Rob Myers kissed me at a dumb party a couple years later. It was a distinct disappointment for both of us, I'm sure. He knew even less about the procedure than I did, but at least I had profited by observing the technique of TV and movie stars. Two people who try to make contact straight on are headed for trouble. Noses are a big factor in the geography of a face, overlooked at your peril. He came at me so quickly the collision left tears in our eyes.

Charlie Bonneville kissed me after an eighth-grade dance. I never really knew why, but I had my dark suspicions. The guys called him Checklist Charlie, so I knew he'd just added my name to a list of girls he'd kissed. I simply couldn't figure why he'd embarked on such a stupid project. It seemed a shame, too, that I couldn't react in the same uncivilized fashion as I had at the age of nine. In a secret poll that year, the girls voted Charlie Bonneville as Most Likely to Grow Up a Degenerate.

Now how could I tell Emily any of that? She'd

just have to find out for herself that the road to sophistication is full of potholes.

Though sorely tempted, I didn't stretch the truth. "No, Jon wasn't the first guy to kiss me. But he's the first one who's—special. I really like him."

"I know." Emily smiled. "I do, too. I think Jon's great."

She finally went off to get into her clown outfit. A few minutes later, Byron wandered in, too late for the family breakfast but earlier than he usually appears on Sunday mornings.

I looked at him and grinned, wondering what he thought about Nicole's curfew, almost as severe as mine.

He startled me by reading my mind. Over a glass of orange juice, he murmured, "Well, at least I'm getting more sleep, home in the sack by midnight." He chuckled. "She's worth it."

"Took the words right out of my mouth," I said. "In fact, that's what I told Jon last night. About me." I filled him in. His accident had caused a sticky situation for me, after all.

Byron surprised me again by apologizing. "I'll see if I can talk Dad out of any heavy-handed stuff," he said. "Jon isn't exactly a wild and crazy kid. He'll be good for you."

Bright blue eyes studied me for a long moment. "I can see the change in you already. You don't stand on your head to get a laugh anymore. And I never thought I'd see the day when you'd come out with a line like that, either. Telling him you were worth it. Took guts. I'm proud of you, you know that?"

A long speech for Byron, and one I never expected to hear. Also, I'm sure he never dreamed he'd end up saying as much as he did. We exchanged faint, embarrassed smiles. Then both of us spoke at the same time.

"I've got a problem," I said.

"I want to ask you something," he said.

I motioned for him to go first.

"Nicole's birthday," he said. "Any ideas about a present? Something she'd really like."

"Byron." I laughed. "It isn't till December. Two whole months away."

He shrugged. "I can be looking, can't I?"

He really had it bad. I was vastly pleased because I knew Nicole was crazy about him, too. "I'll think about it. Maybe she'll mention something she wants. Meg and I never get her clothes or jewelry—she can get that kind of thing at a discount from her mom's shop."

"Yeah." His toast popped up, and Byron reached for it. "So what's your problem?"

I got the butter out and put it on the counter

beside him. Half the time Byron ate his meals there, standing up and gulping his food, always in a hurry to get somewhere, school or football practice. Today he didn't seem to be in a rush. It might be wise to take advantage of a rare opportunity. Byron had time to give me and he seemed to be in a mellow mood.

"It's Foxie. Lorraine Foxworth. You know her?"

Byron glanced at me sharply. "You've tangled with her? She's bad news."

"Tell me about it." But I was the one who had to tell him, beginning with a description of the slice-up-Shelley routine that I found so hard to kick, and how Emily came to my defense at the clown meeting. And about Foxie's threat to get even the next time she bumped into me when I was with Jon.

Byron listened, then pondered the situation as he ate another slice of toast and a bowl of cereal. "You didn't say anything else to her? Just that line about going off to play on Highway 805?"

"That's it."

"No cracks about three-headed Shelley, one blond, one brunette, and one undecided?"

I winced and shook my head.

"Nothing about shaving your knees? Or getting a transfusion of giraffe blood because you want to grow two more inches?"

I chewed my lip. "No."

Byron beamed. "You've come a long way, Shelley Liz."

"Yeah, well. Emily went home with all the honors. But—that bothers me, too. Foxie's one of those girls who work at being mean, and—"

"I wonder why." He looked at me with a puzzled frown. "Good-looking, sharp. But always the act—around guys, anyway. Worse than you, not in your class at all. And she's got a mean streak, all right. What makes a person act like that, somebody who's got everything going for them?"

The question had occurred to me, too, but I'd never really tried to come up with an answer. I threw up my hands, more frustrated than confused. I had enough difficulty finding my own answers. I sure didn't feel qualified to analyze anybody else.

"Don't try to slam her, Shell," Byron said. "She'll take you apart. I can see her doing a number on you in front of people. Not just Jon, a whole crowd. If you're smart, you'll play it cool and quiet. Polite. Dignified."

"What about if I just ask her, 'Foxie, what's your problem'?"

He brightened. "Yeah, that's good. I mean, how's she gonna respond to something like that?"

I moaned softly. "With a sledgehammer, right between my eyes."

"Nah. If she does, just give her the question again."

I thought about it. "You wouldn't use the Gwendolyn angle?"

Byron shook his head.

"She'll be expecting it," I said thoughtfully. "So if I don't hit her with—" I grinned. "Yeah. Get her off balance. Is that what you're saying?"

He gave me a slow grin. "Bull's-eye."

"Thanks," I said. "Thanks a lot. That really helps."

Byron flapped one hand. "You got to the bottom line all by yourself. Hey, you'll handle ole Fox just fine. Wish I could be there to see it."

I had to hurry to get ready then. Luckily, the makeup process had become easier with practice, and my costume was a simple one. It would also be as cool and comfortable as possible on a day with the temperature climbing into the eighties.

I skidded out the door seconds after Mom honked for us out front. She took over the driving for Mrs. Malloncrodt on weekend outings.

At the mall, we found a sizable crowd had gathered. Most of the people didn't pay much attention to the mayor's little speech, or to the photographer taking pictures. Or to the city council members looking self-conscious as they stood behind a length of red ribbon across the main access lane.

Miss Mesa Vista earned a few second glances, though, because she was a fantastically pretty blonde

125

in a low-cut white dress and a rhinestone-studded crown. I watched her smile radiantly for the camera as she held her scissors poised over the ribbon. Once she cut it, there were a few faint cheers, the photographer departed, and Miss Mesa Vista snatched the crown from her head and hurried across the parking lot. Her frown seemed to indicate she might be thinking, Well, *that's* over with.

Why had she entered the contest if she didn't enjoy this kind of thing? Just to get her name and picture in the paper? I decided it must be another case of different strokes. I remembered Byron telling me, "You don't stand on your head to get a laugh anymore." With my record, I sure couldn't throw rocks at Miss Mesa Vista if she needed the spotlight for her own reasons.

Mrs. De Witt met us in front of Penney's, where we'd been told to gather. She wore her clown costume, a goofy approximation of a sailor suit, so she'd chosen the name of Salty.

She grinned at us. "Well, troops, this is D-Day. D for Demonstration. That means demonstrating everything you've learned in the past few weeks. Are you ready?"

A few of us merely nodded, dry mouthed, already perspiring from nerves before we went into action. The rest gave her broad smiles and an echo:

"Ready!" I noted with relief that Foxie hadn't shown up that day.

"Okay, move out around the edges of this big circle. You can peel off by twos or threes when you're ready to do your skits. Remember those folks in Mac's. People like clowns. They're going to look at you and stop and smile. They want to have fun today as much as you do. So—come on, clowns, let's go!"

The stores here had been built around a big courtyard with a fountain in the middle and ringed by benches where people could sit and rest after they'd shopped for a while. Halfway around, Megan spotted a bunch of little kids with their mothers. She headed for them, already digging in her pocket for balloons.

A little farther on, Nicole and I left the main group and did a pantomime we'd discussed on our way to the mall. First, she did her ridiculous soft-shoe dance and I tried to imitate her, falling over my feet. Then she pretended she suddenly realized that people were watching us. Overcome by shyness, she did everything but tuck her head under her arm—and she tried to do that, looking hilarious as she peeked out from under her elbow.

I circled around her, pointing and laughing silently in my role as the showoff, gesturing to the onlookers until they started to laugh, too. Especially when I pretended to stumble over my oversize shoes and landed on my rear, well padded with old towels I'd pinned inside the pants. I had finally learned how to break my fall by getting my hands on the ground before my fanny landed. The tough part was not being obvious.

The skit went really well. Our little audience applauded. As Nicole wandered off, I got to my feet, pulling cards out of my pocket. They were slips of paper or cardboard with idiotic riddles on them.

Why is tennis such a noisy game? Because each player raises a RACKET.

How did the octopus go into battle? Well ARMED.

What did one magnet say to another? My, you're ATTRACTIVE.

What has 2 tails, 6 feet and 2 trunks? An elephant with SPARE PARTS.

"Take a card," I urged in my high Acey-Deucey voice. "Take any card." Almost everyone obliged, glancing at them and chuckling before they went on their way.

I dived into a second group of onlookers, giving out my riddles. Then I felt a tug on my sleeve. A little boy with a gap-toothed grin held out the last bunch of cards.

"Hey, clown, you wanta use these again? Those guys threw 'em away."

I'd planned to pick up the cards later if people ignored the trash cans scattered around the mall. Leave it to a six-year-old to suggest recycling my supply.

"Thanks, Charlie."

"Not Charlie. I'm Kevin."

"Sorry about that." I lowered my voice to a growl. "Thanks, Kevin."

He studied me. "You're a girl, aren't you?"

In those few seconds, another crowd had gathered. Kevin's question brought a ripple of laughter. "I'm Acey Deucey," I told him. "Girl clown— or clown girl. Whichever way you want to look at it."

"Girls can't be clowns." He shook his head. His hazel eyes weren't exactly hostile, but they held a challenge I couldn't ignore.

Abruptly, I became aware of the blazing sun. My head felt wet already beneath my red wig. Mrs. De Witt had never warned us about moments like this. Megan could have the kids, I thought darkly. The pinchers, the shin kickers, and budding chauvinists like this one. She could take them all—preferably a thousand miles away from me.

"Hey, little lady!" a fat man called from the front row of onlookers. "The kid just said girls can't be clowns. What do you say to that?"

I took a deep breath, but it didn't help. Maybe

the Santa Ana was to blame. All I can say is, I went slightly crazy.

"What do I say?" I smiled until I thought my face would split, knowing my clown mouth would make that silly grin look even wider, and certainly a lot happier than I felt. I did a little capering dance, ending with one foot in midair.

"I say, lay-deeze and gen-tul-men, can't you believe the evidence of your own eyes?" I made it a chant. "Do you have twenty-twenty vision? Can't you see the proof before you in full livid color? My name is Acey Deucey, and I'M A CLOWN!"

The moment I paused, Kevin repeated the only argument he had: "You're only a girl." He must have figured it would be enough to win the day.

More laughter from the crowd, growing by the minute, attracted by an unexpected dialogue between one pint-size fiend and one perspiring clown, girl variety. I felt strongly tempted to turn in my tubes of Clown Red, White, and Black on the spot. But at that extraordinarily painful moment, for the second time I recalled Byron's advice.

Would that work with a macho in miniature? He stood eyeing me with a broad grin, the devil in his eyes.

I played it cool and I played it quiet, but with broad gestures. Damn it, I thought, I *am* a clown. Bending forward, hands on knees, head to one side, compassion in my voice, I asked, "What's the matter, Kevin? You want to be a clown, too? Well, you can be. All you have to do is grow up a little more. Then, if you join a class and learn all about clowning, you can do what all these clowns are doing today. That's what makes you a clown. It's not who you are. It's what you do."

For the first time, he looked confused. Some of the people around him clapped. Kevin must have decided he'd lost the battle. He ducked into the crowd and disappeared.

I barely had time to sigh with relief before Nicole came running from the other side of the courtyard. "Come quick! You can't miss this! Wait'll you see what Megan's doing!"

We went around the edges of the audience to a planter in front of the shoe store. I wondered at the silence, broken only by occasional laughter and spurts of applause. When I saw Megan, I gaped for a moment, then clutched Nicole's arm.

"I know," she said softly. "Isn't she wonderful?"

It startled me most, I think, to see Megan working with a partner, a skinny little guy only a couple inches taller than she. Like a lot of traditional mimes, he wore a tightfitting black costume with gloves. His makeup was whiteface with exaggerated black brows, a red mouth outlined in black, and only a few vertical lines above and below his eyes.

131

As I watched, he went through what must have been his regular act, walking an invisible dog, getting tangled in the leash, trying to get the dog to climb some stairs.

Megan went along as if they'd been practicing for weeks. The mime had problems every time he tried to get the dog to obey. Megan had none. Each time the little guy hopped away to tear his hair in frustration, he turned to see Megan accomplish what he'd failed to do. Then she'd dust her hands together and look at him brightly as if to say, "Okay, now what?"

"How long have they been doing this?" I asked Nicole. "Who is he, anyway?"

"Haven't the vaguest idea. He came by a few minutes ago, watched Megan working with some kids and—they started doing this kind of thing. He hasn't said a word to her, far as I could tell. She just picked up what he wanted and—aren't they terrific?"

We didn't find out the whole story until hours later. Megan didn't have lunch with us, but she sent Emily to tell us she'd meet us at the car around three.

Emily said, her eyes sparkling through her ludicrous Cricket makeup, "His name's Mark Mahoney. They're having lunch at the restaurant over on Woodlawn." She looked a little anxious. "He'll pay for it, won't he?"

Nicole and I giggled.

"He'd better," Nicole said. "Prices are pretty high in there. Megan's a lucky dog. I bet it's air-conditioned, too."

After Emily went to sit with her friends at another table, Nicole smiled at me. "Can you believe that? I mean, it looks like this guy's just freaked over Megan. How are we ever going to wait until three o'clock to find out?"

Jon and Byron arrived after lunch and stayed for an hour or so. They brought us Cokes with lots of ice and clapped like crazy when we did our skit. I learned a lot that day. But by the time we headed for the car, I felt as if I'd been on a runaway roller coaster.

At least we ended the afternoon on a high note. Megan tried to answer all our questions at once. Mark Mahoney was a sophomore at the Catholic high school. He wanted Megan to work as his part-ner. He'd been a mime for over a year, working first with his brother, who was now away at college. He and Megan had talked for two hours over lunch.

Then she said, her eyes dismayed in her funny hobo-face, "I didn't think— I simply never thought at the time— Oh, it's the silliest thing—"

"What? What?"

"He wants me to meet him for lunch next Saturday. At the same place."

"Well, great. Fine. Wonderful. What's the problem?"

"Without our makeup," she said, "how'll we know each other?"

Nicole and I collapsed against each other, hysterical.

"And that's not the worst part—"

"Oh, Megan, what? What else?"

"When he sees me without my makeup, maybe—maybe he won't like me anymore."

"Megan, you silly twit." I couldn't help laughing even though she looked so mournful, her own mouth downturned along with that of the huge unhappy clown mouth that surrounded it.

"There you are, made up as a scruffy tramp—red nose, enormous mouth, even a beard. You think the real you won't be an improvement over that?"

Her nose twitched. She giggled. And finally all three of us roared with laughter.

10

The rainy season began in late November that year, a couple of days before Thanksgiving. Emily and I made dinner the night before the holiday so Mom could start on the pies and her cranberry-orange relish that I love with turkey.

We fixed what we call E.G.I.I. soup—Everything Goes In It—scraps of meat and vegetables in a base of stock. It's always good, but it can vary from adequate to delicious, depending on the leftovers we find in the refrigerator.

I had to keep an eye on Emily. She's inclined to get carried away. This time I caught her seconds before she dumped half a can of salmon in the pot.

"No!" I yelped. Once the dish was safely in my grasp, I closed my eyes and shuddered. "Emily, you can indulge your spirit of adventure on your own ghastly sandwiches. Do you want the whole family to come down with food poisoning the night before Thanksgiving?"

Mom rolled her eyes, but Emily just laughed. "Nobody around here ever wants to try anything new. Hey, a little salmon flavor might be great."

"Gross, more likely," Mom murmured. She went back to her pie crust, looking adorable with a smudge of flour on her chin. "You girls better make some sandwiches to go with the soup. Byron feels abused if he doesn't get at least three thousand calories in one sitting." She glanced at Emily and added firmly, "Toasted cheese sandwiches would be fine."

Emily sighed. "Okay. He'll just have to wait till tomorrow to pig out."

At dinner, Byron seemed unusually quiet. I studied him, wondering if something was bothering him. Then Mom and Dad started talking, and I concentrated on E.G.I.I. soup. It had turned out really good this time.

When I glanced up, I saw Dad look at Emily, then at Mom. They both smiled. "Our little one's growing up," Dad commented. "She hasn't said a word all during dinner."

Emily grinned and turned pink.

Underneath her reply to Dad, Mom said to me, softly, "She has somebody to talk to now, doesn't she?"

It jolted me. I realized she was right. Emily talked to *me* these days. Or rather, we talked to each other. Not all the time, but a whole lot more than we ever did before. One of us had sure changed.

Emily didn't ask personal questions very often, either. When she came out with something really outrageous, I'd glare at her. Then she'd laugh and say, "I just wanted to see if you were paying attention."

Actually, it was kind of fun comparing notes with her about the teachers I'd had in junior high. And the way a lot of the boys still act like sixth-grade wimps. Well, some of the girls, too. And Emily couldn't wait to meet Mrs. Upjohn because I'd quoted her theory about everybody following a unique growing-up schedule.

About an hour after dinner, Byron came back to my room, and it turned out I'd been right about something bothering him. Naturally, I didn't feel happy about that, but it did please me that I'd picked up on the fact that something might be wrong.

He sat down on the rug, his back against the closet door, and glowered at me. "I had a long talk with Granny Gus this afternoon," he said.

"Oh? I thought Nicole went shopping."

Byron nodded. "Granny set it up. She wanted to talk to me alone."

"About going to Sunnyside?"

"Yeah. Her doctor's putting on the pressure. So's Nicole's Mom." His glower turned into a frown. "She only checks on Granny about once a month, Nicky says, just long enough to get everybody all shook. But she's pushing this Sunnyside Home thing, and for once Granny agrees with her. It's Nicky who goes up the wall if you mention it."

"I know." I sighed. "Remember I told you Granny talked to Meg and me a while back? She wanted us to make sure Nicole goes along when the clowns go out to the Home."

"When's that?"

"In a couple weeks. But Nicky says she won't go. Even if she does, I don't see what good it'll do. She won't even learn to drive so she can go see Granny when—"

Byron made a brief gesture. "I'm taking care of that. I've been giving her lessons." Amusement flickered in his eyes. "Hasn't she mentioned it?"

"No." I gave a startled laugh. "How's she doing?"

He shrugged. "She's a natural. And you can't go far wrong with a car like Granny's. Volvos aren't that big, but they're heavy, good balance. With power steering and all the extras, no problem. She'll be driving like a pro in no time."

"That's good."

"Thing is, she's still hung up on this Sunnyside deal. Would it be a good idea to talk to her? I mean, a really heavy session, laying it on her, what's gonna happen. What has to happen. Would she—would she face it then?"

I flopped across my bed, propped my pillow under my chin, and stared at him. "It'd be—one bad trip," I said at last. "She might really freak. Turn on you." I bit my lip. "Tell you the truth, Megan and I, we've thought about talking to her like that, too. We always chicken out, decide to wait and see—"

"Time's running out," Byron said soberly. He pounded his knee with his fist. "Granny says after the first of the year, she's gonna go to Sunnyside. She wants Nicole to have one more Christmas just like always, and then—"

"Wow." I swallowed hard. "Byron, you want me to talk to her?" I saw the way he smiled at me, and my heart felt squeezed and sore.

"Nah. Appreciate the offer, but—all I wanted to know was if you think it's a good idea."

"I do. But you're risking an awful lot, Byron. It might help Nicole, sure, if you—if you force her to face facts. But she might never forgive you for it. Honestly, I don't know how she'd react."

Byron put one big hand on the floor and pushed himself to his feet. I've seen him do it at least fifty times and it's clearly impossible, but he doesn't know that, I guess. "Okay, thanks."

"For what? I didn't help at all."

He gave me the smile again. "Yeah, you did." At the door he turned, his hand on the knob. "Another thing. I know what to get for her birthday."

"You do? What?"

"A puppy. One of the guys at the store has a pedigreed shepherd. She has eight pups. They'll be ready to leave their mama any day now."

"That's terrific," I said. "She'll love a puppy."

"It'll help with the other problem, too."

"How?"

Byron grinned. "Nicole's a very conscientious girl. Crazy about animals. Puppies, kittens, you name it. Right?"

"Yeah. So?"

"So a puppy's gonna keep her mighty busy. Housebreaking it, feeding it, exercising it. It's also a *big* dog. A big dog needs a lot of exercise. Has to be trained, disciplined, or it's a pain in the rear."

He laughed. "I already checked with Granny and Tilly. They think it's a great idea to keep Nicky busy, keep her mind off things. I just—I just hope it works."

"Me, too." I added quietly, "Byron? You still think she's worth it?"

"I know she's worth it," he said. Then he went out, closing the door behind him.

It stopped raining during the night, and a pale, watery sun shone on Thanksgiving Day. It didn't warm the sharp wind, but at least it looked less depressing when I glanced out the kitchen window. As we went full speed ahead toward the humongous holiday dinner, maddening smells from the roasting turkey and spicy pies filled the kitchen and drifted into the rest of the house.

Dad and Byron built a fire in the fireplace while Emily and I set the table with Mom's best linen cloth and the good china and silver, even the goblets that we use on special occasions. They had been my Grandmother Avery's, and my mother's really sentimental about them. I suppose they bring back memories of holidays when she was little.

Thanksgiving Day turned out to be one of those that I consciously record at the time, aware that someday I'll look back and think, Yes, that was a total 10.

I went for a long walk with Jon in the afternoon, but not to work up an appetite. We were both restless after being cooped up indoors by a week of constant rain. It would have been nice to work out with our ongoing, over-the-hedge tennis game. But the ground was still soggy in back, so we walked instead, holding hands and only talking when we felt like it.

He came back that evening after we'd all eaten to play cards with Mom and Dad and Emily and me. Byron was over at Nicole's, of course. I had a kind of bittersweet feeling about that, knowing my brother would be heading for college and a life apart from the family in another year. Now that we had become closer, the knowledge bothered me a lot more than it once had.

Megan called the next day to ask if Emily and I would like to do a special clown thing at the hospital on Saturday. "In the children's ward," she said. "Mark's going to be there, and Mrs. De Witt said any of the clowns can go. Some of them don't want to go out to Sunnyside in two weeks, so—"

"Nicole, for one," I said unhappily. "The last time I asked about it, she wouldn't even answer me. Have you had any luck?"

"No. She's going to the hospital tomorrow, though. Want us to pick you up?"

"Sure. You don't want my Mom to drive?"

Megan laughed. "My mother's crazy about Mark. I told you that. But she's never seen him perform. She's watched us practice, but it's better in full makeup. You know. So she jumped at the chance to go this time. Dad's going to take my brothers to their game. We worked it all out."

"Good." I grinned, recalling how I used to worry about the time when Megan would start dating. I never dreamed Mrs. Malloncrodt would act like this, so pleased with Megan's choice of boyfriends that her little brothers didn't always get the lion's share of attention.

As it turned out, I came close to canceling the hospital trip myself. Byron came in the back door just before we sat down to a meal of leftovers from yesterday's feast. One look at his face and I knew what had happened. My heart gave a sickening lurch, then thudded heavily in my chest.

"You're just in time, Byron," Mom said. Peering into the oven, she didn't see his face.

"I'm not hungry, Mom. Maybe I'll grab something later." He headed toward the hall.

"Not *hungry*?" She straightened and looked at me, bewildered.

"It's Nicole," I whispered, and took off after him.

He stood just inside his room, waiting for me. "I took the puppy over to her," he said, his voice harsh, "and afterward we—we talked. She went up like a rocket. Never wants to see me again."

He took a deep breath, and his throat moved convulsively. "I don't know what it'll take—to get through to her. Gave it my best shot. Didn't work, that's all."

"Oh, Byron—"

143

He gave me a ghastly smile. "Well, I knew it was a gamble. I suppose I'd— Yeah, if I had it to do over, I'd do the same thing. That's a great old lady there. Nicky doesn't see how rough she's making it—for everybody." He shook his head. "She just can't see it."

"I'm—I'm really sorry."

"Yeah, well. Thanks." He closed the door.

But the pain on his face had been etched into my mind. Hours later, on the edge of sleep, it came back to jar me fully awake again. I knew then that I'd have to talk to Nicole, too. Even if it meant the end of our friendship.

11

The next afternoon, Emily and I climbed into the backseat of the car with Megan. Nicole was in front with Mrs. Malloncrodt, so I relaxed a little. If I didn't sit by Nicole, maybe nobody would notice the strain between us.

She glanced back at me, then looked away quickly and began to talk to Megan's mother. No one seemed to pick up on any unusual tension. I munched nervously on some peanuts I found in my pocket, glad I hadn't said anything to Megan or Emily. It hadn't seemed wise, especially after I had decided to talk to Nicole myself.

The minute we parked in the hospital lot, Nicole

145

got out and hurried to join the group standing by the side door with Mrs. De Witt. Then Mark Mahoney came over to meet us, and Mrs. Malloncrodt burbled over his costume and makeup while Megan and Emily looked on with broad grins. Nobody paid any attention to Nicole's abrupt departure.

In the lobby, one of the Pink Ladies greeted us and said she'd be our hostess for the next couple of hours. As usual, we created quite a stir. Visitors slumped in chairs looked up from their magazines and away from the TV to stare at the sudden invasion of clowns. Then they gave us amiable smiles.

On our way to the elevators, passing nurses hailed us cheerfully. "Hi, clowns, where you going?"

"The children's ward," we chorused.

"Come see us afterward," a pretty redhead coaxed. "Second floor. Lots of old folks up there. They'll just love you."

In spite of myself, I turned and found Nicole staring at me. Our eyes met for one sizzling second before she turned away. I couldn't be sure, but even with her Bubble Bum makeup, her eyes looked puffy, as if she'd been crying.

Our group piled out of the elevator on the third floor and waited a few minutes until Mrs. De Witt arrived with the rest of our troops. She counted noses and suggested we go off by twos and threes, as we'd done before.

"Remember, we'll only go to the rooms the nurses have on our list. Some of these kids are too sick for visitors."

She held up her hand as Pom-Pom and Fiddle-Faddle moved a few steps away. "A word of caution. Approach the children slowly. You don't want to scare them. Remember what you've been taught. The costumes and makeup can startle them at first, so use a hand puppet, shake hands, give them a balloon, do a magic trick. Speak softly and play it by ear. Okay?"

For a few minutes, I wondered why I'd agreed to participate. Up to now, my experience with kids hadn't left me with any warm and tender feelings. Kevin and Bethie had both left scars that made me wary of further contact with the lollipop set. So I stayed close to Mark and Megan for the first hour.

I soon found that these kids were wonderful. Recovering from broken bones or surgery, bored with their stay in the hospital, they laughed and cheered at everything we did. So did the visiting relatives in every room.

One boy with a mop of sandy curls seemed fascinated with the mimes. He urged Mark and Megan to repeat their walking-the-dog routine over and over. A giggly little Mexican girl loved my riddles and begged for extra cards. I had a hunch she'd try them out on the nurses. We left her studying them and muttering to herself, "Why are you so tired on April Fool's Day? Because you've had a thirty-one-day MARCH!"

The peanuts I'd eaten had made me thirsty, so I told Megan I'd catch up with her later and went in search of a drinking fountain. On my way back, somebody called to me from one of the rooms.

"Hey, clown! Hey, you *clown*! Come here a minute, willya?"

I hesitated and checked the door, but there wasn't a NO VISITORS sign. No visitors, either, to talk to the tiny girl lying in bed with one of her legs in a cast and held aloft in traction.

She looked about eight, but my guess could have been off by a couple of years either way. The fat chestnut braids and sharp features in a small thin face didn't offer any clues.

"Hi," I said, and waited for a smile or some other signal to indicate whether she wanted company or a private show. "What's your name?"

"Samantha. Call me Sam." No smile. Her eyes were more green than gray, and there were dark circles like bruises underneath them.

I drew in a breath, reading in those eyes something I'd glimpsed only rarely in the past. One of my aunts looks like that when she has a raging migraine headache. And Granny Gus's eyes give her

148

away when her arthritis is bad. Samantha-Call-Me-Sam was clearly hurting a lot.

She let out her breath in a loud sigh. "I was so scared none of you would come back. The nurse said you'd be here today, and then I saw you go on by. Must have just waked up from a nap. I never sleep very long at a time. And I thought, wow, I'd missed you. Clowns! Lucky you came along—"

I dragged over a chair so she could see me without moving her head. "So how'd you bust your leg, Sam? Tangle with a runaway truck?"

A faint smile. "Nah. Fell off the parallel bars at school. Talk about dumb."

"Happens. You're looking at the klutz of the Charles R. Mayfair School. Never broke a bone, but I'd hate to tell you how many times I sprained something. Or cut myself. Used to leave a trail of blood from the far end of the playground to the nurse's office. The kids would half carry me through the door and the nurse would say, 'You again.' All through kindergarten I figured she thought that was my *name*. You again."

Samantha almost laughed this time. "I'm like that, too. My Dad says I'm accident prone."

The way she said it, I figured her father often told her that, probably in the same resigned tone of voice. So I quoted my marvelous Molly Marine

149

again, simplifying the details about eye-hand co-ordination just enough to let Sam know she'd out-grow the stage where she tripped over her feet every five minutes.

"How old are you, anyway?"

"Ten."

"My sister Emily's eleven."

"I bet she thinks it's neat what you're doing. Boy, just like real clowns, magic tricks and everything." For a moment, the green eyes lost their pain-glazed expression.

"Got news for you," I said. "Emily's a clown, too. She's Cricket. I'm Acey Deucey. Here, want a card?"

She chose one from the dozen fanned out in my hand and read it aloud, slowly. "What do you call a man who steals hamburgers? A HAMBURGLAR." Sam groaned and giggled. "How old are you, Acey Deucey?"

"Fifteen."

She lifted her head to stare at me. "It's hard to tell what you look like. *Who's in there?*"

She said it in an odd, intent tone that gave me goose bumps for a second. But she went on quickly, her voice warming as she spoke.

"All that stuff on your face—must take a long time to put it on. I love the little hearts and dia-monds. But I can tell, you're actually very pretty. It's funny, though, covering up who you really are.

150

Hiding under all that white glop and—and that awful red wig. It's like Halloween. Only you can dress up anytime, can't you?"

I almost blurted out something really stupid, that I'd been covering up—maybe hiding would be a better word—for a long time. I'd been a Funny Girl practically all my life. Then I told myself firmly that Sam needed therapy a whole lot more than I did. She'd been lying here hurting with nobody to visit her.

My tongue went into action without checking with the department upstairs. "Are your parents coming in today?"

Her head moved against the pillow. Negative. "My dad travels," Sam said. "He's only home every other weekend. And Mom—well, she's been really good, but actually she hates hospitals. It's a—what do you call it?—some kind of phobia, she says." She made a face. "I'm coming down with it myself. Boy, I'll have the worst case ever by the time they let me out of here."

My blood had come to a slow simmer. I felt grateful for the makeup that would hide my opinion of Sam's supersensitive mom. "Well!" I said brightly. "What do you say I go round up the rest of the clowns to do their stuff for you? I want you to meet Emily. Got a feeling you two will hit it off and—we can come visit again, you know. Listen, Samantha

151

Sam, when you see us without our makeup, you're in for a *real* shock."

She laughed out loud. "Hey, that'd be great."

I hurried down the hall toward the sound of laughter in one of the rooms at the end. On the way I stopped a nurse and asked how long Sam would be in the hospital.

Her face tightened. "A week, maybe longer. That leg's broken in two places and one of those breaks is *bad*." She smiled at me. "I'm so glad you went in to see her. She'd been sleeping and—sleep's a sometime thing for Sam. I didn't want to disturb her even for you kids, though I knew you'd do her a world of good. Her mommy's a tender violet, finds all of this just too upsetting. Sam's lucky if that darling person shows up every other day."

"Yeah, I picked up on that."

She took a deep breath. "I'm talking out of turn, I guess." She patted my shoulder. "It'd be wonderful if you'd come to visit again. Sam needs all the help she can get."

I went to bring the clowns back to put on a show for Sam. By the time we left, her face had come alive with a smile and a lot of color, especially when Emily and I promised we'd come to see her again.

Mrs. De Witt counted us again at the elevator. "We'll spend a half hour down on the second floor," she said. "Oh, dear, somebody's missing."

"Nicole went back to the car." Megan glanced at me and lifted one shoulder. The gesture said clearly, *That figures.*

My blood pressure went up a few more degrees. "I'd like to beg off, too, Mrs. De Witt."

She looked at me closely. "You all right, Shelley? Some of these kids—they can get to you—"

"It's not that." I tried to sound casual. "I want to talk to Nicole—about going out to Sunnyside."

She nodded and stepped aside as the elevator door opened behind her.

On the way down, Megan whispered, "Are you sure you don't want to wait till I'm there, too? You know Nicole. And she's been acting really weird today."

So Megan had noticed the tension after all. I might have known. She's so tuned in, almost nothing gets by her. "No big thing. I just want to talk to her."

The rest of them got off at the second floor. The last thing I saw before the door closed were Megan's eyes peering anxiously out of her absurd Patches makeup.

I found Nicole sitting on the planter at one edge of the parking lot. "Decided you'd sit this one out, huh?"

There wasn't any note of accusation in my voice, but she stiffened. "Guess I had enough for one

153

day," she said. "Ah—Shelley, I suppose Byron told you about—about—"

"Yeah."

She looked down at her oversize shoes and traced a lopsided circle with one heel. "I want you to know— I hope it won't change our friendship. The way you and I feel about each other, I don't want this to— to make a difference."

"Sorry," I said. "It does make a difference. What you did to my brother—how can you possibly think that won't change the way I feel about you?" My voice shook. In fact, I realized I was trembling all over. Talking to Sam must have made all my nerve endings more sensitive. I don't think I'd ever felt a raw anger like that.

Nicole said remotely, her head still bent, "It doesn't concern you. For that matter, what Byron said— it's something that doesn't concern him, either."

"Doesn't concern him? Of course it does. You're— you were his girl. And he loves Granny, too. So does Megan. So do I. We've all seen what's happening—because of that blind spot of yours. Byron had the guts to do something about it. He tried to help. I never wanted to risk spoiling our friendship, and I guess Megan didn't, either. So what does that tell you?"

A short, tense silence. A siren wailed in the distance. Then it came closer, cutting off as an am-

154

bulance turned in from the street and went by the side of the building.

Nicole hunched one shoulder, her cheek against the rough material of her checked jacket. The red flower in her little hat sagged toward her curly gray wig.

"It tells me—you and Megan—you know me better than—than he does. So you had sense enough to keep your mouths shut." She still held her head to one side. A tear crossed the bridge of her nose and plopped on the ground.

I felt my anger drain away. What did I know about the reasons people act the way they do? It just seemed so dumb, the way Nicole was hitting out at the people she loved the most.

"It's—such a waste," I said, more to myself than to her. "Here we are, blasting away at each other. And you took Byron apart, too. And Granny's just as miserable as he is."

At the moment, it seemed vital to complete the list of things that grieved me. "And there's a poor little kid up there—her name is Sam—with a mother who's a real crumb. Won't even come to visit because hospitals depress her."

Nicole looked up at me, confused. "What?" she said. "What's that little kid got to do with—"

I took two steps toward the car. "It just seems to me, the main thing in life is—you should be there for other people when they need you. Same as you'd want them to be there for you.

"We had that figured out way back in third grade, Nicole. Remember? First Friends Forever. So where's Sam's mom when she needs her? And right now, when Granny Gus needs you most, where are you?"

Nicole looked even more bewildered.

"Why can't I make you see that you're so wrapped up in yourself you don't care about anyone else!" My voice was so harsh, it hurt my throat. "Granny's getting desperate. She's even turning to us kids— Megan and me. And Byron. Anybody she thinks you might listen to. I should have had enough class to tackle you first before you shot my brother down. I might have been able to help, but I didn't even try. I won't be able to forget that. Ever."

Nicole stared at me, stunned.

I turned and walked quickly to the car. I'd tried, but too late. Now I'd only made things worse.

12

With one exception, in the days that followed, it seemed as if everything in my life had begun to fall into place. Jon and I were so comfortable with each other, anybody would have thought we'd been dating for a long time. I felt more confident about school, too, especially after the first report card came out. My grades were fine, even a B in P.E.!

Mrs. Upjohn patted my shoulder when I thanked her and said briskly, "Way to go, Lucas. Wish everybody tried as hard as you do. You're burning up the track."

The one cloud amidst all this dazzling sunshine was the rift with Nicole. My parents were upset about it but cautious about offering advice. Dad tried to sound optimistic, saying things like, "Hey, honey, it'll work out—" But it was clear he couldn't be sure of that himself.

Mom just commented unhappily, "Sweetie, I just don't know what to tell you—"

They couldn't come up with more than that, and I was glad they didn't try. The important thing was showing that they cared about the problem Byron and I shared, one that wouldn't be solved easily and quickly, if ever.

Emily felt really bad about it, too. "Let me know if you think I can help—"

Byron still couldn't talk about the situation at any length. But one night he said, "I think it's great that you talked to Nicole, but—I wish you hadn't. I mean, it messed up your friendship."

"Couldn't be helped. Some things just had to be said."

He nodded. "Well—thanks, anyway." He went off, leaving me feeling faintly comforted.

Megan seemed as distressed as the three people most affected. Unable to bring about a reconciliation, she did the next best thing, in her view. She talked to Nicole herself.

"Megan," I said, "it's a wonder she didn't get mad at you, too. I may be ticked off at her, but I'm still aware that she needs *somebody* at this point."

158

We were talking on the phone that night, and Megan sounded tired and frustrated. "No, she didn't yell and holler at me at all. But I didn't accomplish anything, either. She only cried. And told me over and over, 'I'm just not ready.' What could I say after that?"

"I probably would have said a whole lot. Too much, for sure. And none of it would have helped. Thing is, a person almost never *is* ready for big terrible changes. You know? Maybe it's a matter of being together enough so when something happens, you *don't* fall apart."

Even as I said the words, they sounded smug. Comments like that are bound to challenge fate. I never seem to learn that lesson, though, even after the dozens of times I've ended up mopping egg off my face.

As a result, on that Friday night two weeks later I didn't have a suspicion that a crisis hovered, awaiting an opportunity to drop on me like a bomb. School had let out that day for the Christmas break, and holiday spirit warmed me. It was a lovely glow I often wish I could bottle to take like vitamins the rest of the year.

Jon and I went to the early show at the shopping center. The movie turned out to be a real loser, one of those flicks that irritate the audience so much that people talk back to the actors on the screen.

We left early to beat the crowd to Farrell's and tore the movie apart over hot fudge sundaes.

Once we'd done that, Jon asked, "Are you gonna see that little kid again tomorrow?"

"No, Sam went home last week." I told him what the nurse had said. " 'She actually had mixed feelings about that, Shelley. She said, "Boy, I'll miss those clowns, especially Acey Deucey. Every time she came to see me, I forgot how much I hurt." You know what she said then? "I loved Acey Deucey, but I think I like Shelley even better." ' "

I smiled at him. "I sure felt good about that." Finishing the last of the whipped cream on my sundae, I started on the ice cream. "Sam's sure a neat little kid. I'll never forget the first day when she kind of squinted at me and said, *Who's in there?*' It gave me the shivers. As if she could see clear through to—to the person I really am."

I studied Jon for a minute. A lock of red hair had fallen over one eyebrow, and I hoped he wouldn't brush it back. In that moment, I could see exactly what he must have looked like when he was little.

"In a way, that's what you did, Jon. Back in my hyper days, I mean. You seemed to know it was all an act. Remember? You told me one day if I stopped going for the laughs I'd find out I was good at a lot of things. You're the first person—outside my family and Megan and Nicole—who ever saw *me*.

Way down deep, I guess I figured nobody would notice how totally inadequate I was—if I made them laugh. But I didn't know for a long time what I was doing. Not until I joined the clown class."

Jon grinned and flipped one hand in an easy gesture. "You were never a totally inadequate person. As Coach Daley would say, 'You were not living up to your potential.' " He made a wry face. Jon and Coach Daley have a prickly relationship at best.

"I used to watch you in class," he said, "and make up these stories in my head. How somebody would try to kidnap you, and I'd race to the rescue, flattening the guy with one punch. And then you'd throw your arms around me and tell me how great I was, and—" He stopped, looking a little hurt, when I burst out laughing.

"No, no, no. You don't understand," I said at last. "I'm laughing because—I used to fantasize about *you*. All the time. I dragged you out of burning buildings and saved you from drowning, and—and—I can't believe this. You mean you did the same thing about me?"

He beamed. Then he asked, absurdly, "Shelley, will you marry me? Oh, not for ten years. Maybe fifteen. How can it hurt to get my bid in early?"

Over his shoulder I saw Nicole come in with two girls from the clown class. Jon must have seen my face change. He glanced back and made a soft neutral sound before he returned his attention to his sundae.

I didn't look directly at Nicole again. Out of the corner of my eye, I saw the three of them settle in a booth down the aisle. Nicole sat with her back to me, so I had a hunch she'd seen us.

By the time I finished my ice cream, the place had filled up with all the stubborn people who'd stayed to see the end of that crummy movie. Most of them were kids from school. As they went by our booth, Jon and I teased them about going to ridiculous lengths to get their money's worth.

Laughing at one guy's bitter comment, "Even the pits have pits," I looked toward the door. My heart went *whomp* and started beating like crazy. Foxie had come in with another blond girl.

It wouldn't do a bit of good to try to hide in Jon's pocket. Foxie saw me at the same instant I spotted her. She came down the aisle toward us, her smile growing as she approached.

"Well, if it isn't Acey Deucey," she said in a high clear voice intended to attract attention. "The model for all the clowns around. Because she looks funny even *before* she puts on all that makeup."

Time seemed to stop as I stared up at her. Jon made one sharp movement, then sat quite still. I didn't look at him, but I knew he was watching me. Later I thought I'd imagined the sudden hush, as

162

if everyone in the nearby booths had stopped talking to listen. Jon told me afterward that that's just what they did.

So a sizable audience heard me find my voice. "What're you trying to prove, Foxie?" Not the most brilliant comeback in recorded history. But my tone was perfect, quiet, and even faintly curious.

Her blue eyes widened, startled. Then she recaptured her fading smile. "Not trying to prove a thing, A.D. Just wondering when you plan to take the act on the road."

I ignored that. "It isn't important, anyway, whatever it is you're trying to do. I figure it's your problem, Foxie."

The other blonde tugged impatiently at Foxie's arm, then turned and hurried up the aisle.

"You're the one with the problem, A.D.," Foxie drawled. "And maybe Jon Harrington has a few hang-ups, too. Anybody who goes with Shelley Lucas can't have a really classy self-image. You know?"

I've never been sure when Jon began to speak. I felt anger explode inside, so probably it didn't register for a few seconds that his voice had replaced Foxie's. He sounded as matter-of-fact as if we were alone.

"—so I got to wondering what old Super Jock would say if I told him straight out, 'Listen, coach, if this team doesn't get the league title, if we don't even come close, I won't lose five minutes' sleep—' "

"Jon, would you stay out of this?" Foxie snapped.

"—because there's one thing I won't do once I leave Mesa High, and that's play football. Or basketball. Or baseball. Maybe I'll swim or play tennis, but—"

"Jon, I said—"

"—no more team sports. Ever."

The moment he paused, I picked it up. "Why don't you wait till the day before you graduate? Tell him then. Though I doubt very much—"

The last few words were drowned by a rising wave of sound. Around us, the kids cheered and clapped. Some of them were on their feet, craning their necks to see over the booth so they could look straight at Foxie while they laughed and applauded and whistled.

Her face turned scarlet. She whirled around, looking for her friend, then went on to the end of the aisle and ducked into the ladies' room. Probably she regretted it the moment she realized she'd have to run the gauntlet again when she emerged, passing the booths full of kids who'd laughed at her.

It took several minutes before the place settled down. Jon and I sat, a little stunned, listening to congratulations from all sides.

"Beautiful! About time that chop artist got chopped herself—"

"Hey, you two, lotsa class!"

"That'll show the Fox!"

"She'll think twice before she does another number on you, Shelley!"

When they finally subsided, I let out my breath in a long sigh. Then I reached for Jon's hand. Mine was trembling. His felt like ice. "I think I'll accept your proposal," I said softly. "I'll wait ten years. Or fifteen. So if you'll just kindly put something in writing or on tape, maybe—"

"Sure," he said. But he kept watching me, not a spark of amusement in those dark green eyes.

"You know something?" I said, looking at our hands, not at him. "It's unreal, but—listen, I feel sorry for her. I can't help it. That was awful, what the kids did to her."

"Yeah."

I looked up to see that he was quite serious. "You feel sorry for her, too?"

"Well—just a little." He held up his other hand, thumb and forefinger a fraction of an inch apart, measuring graphically the amount of compassion he'd been able to muster.

"I'm glad you started talking when you did," I said. "When she started in on you—I might have

165

done something really dumb. Like pull out her hair to find out if she'd still be gorgeous—bald."

Jon laughed. "I promised Byron I'd keep my mouth shut and let you handle her—up to a point. He's the one who warned me I'd have to hold you down if Foxie turned the gun on me. Hey, I *like* girls who help fight my battles—"

I dropped his hand. Then I broke up. "You're worth it," I said. "Anybody who lets me beat him at tennis—"

"Got news for you. I'm not letting you beat me. You're doing it all by yourself."

We kicked that around for a few minutes. Just as we decided we'd better leave, a couple of girls, breathless with laughter, came out of the ladies' room and headed toward our booth.

"Oh, Shell, it's one for the record books! So *funny*! You know what's happened to old Foxie?"

"Now what?"

The other girl took over. "Her zipper broke, that's what. And you know how tight her jeans are? She's gonna be stuck in there till the place closes. No coat, no sweater, nothing to hide behind—"

"Where's her friend?"

"That's her cousin. She split, I guess. They were fighting even before they got here. And there's Foxie, begging everybody for a safety pin—as if anybody'd give her one—"

166

When they left, I looked at Jon.

He shrugged. "You got a safety pin?"

I took a deep breath. "No, but I know somebody who does. Nicole." Insecure girls always carry stuff like safety pins. A boy without sisters couldn't be expected to know something like that. "I guess—I guess I'll have to ask her."

"Yeah," Jon said. His eyes were warm. "I suppose you'll have to do that." Then he grinned. "I'll meet you outside."

At Nicole's booth, I said hi to the other girls and pretended I didn't notice how awkward their smiles were. "Hey, Nicole, can I borrow a safety pin?"

She looked at me for a long moment. "I hear Foxie's got a problem. But after what she just did to you—"

"She's been dumped on enough for one day."

Abruptly, Nicole smiled. "I'd better come with you. She'll never believe you'd bail her out. Knowing Foxie, she'll think you dipped that pin in poison or something." She put some money on the table. "You guys want to pay for me? I'll be just a couple minutes."

She followed me back to the ladies' room and we waited as three girls came out, laughing. Foxie was alone. She turned from the washbowl to glare at us. The extent of the disaster was all too clear. Once her zipper conked out, a front zipper at that, a great deal of Foxie had been released from close confinement. No way could she hide something like that on the long walk across Farrell's to the front door.

Silently, Nicole rummaged in her bag, came up with a couple of pins and handed them over. Foxie's face revealed a number of conflicting emotions, but she took the pins. They didn't do the job. The zipper in those jeans had died after truly noble service.

Foxie moaned softly. Up to then, nobody had made a sound.

"Well." I sighed. "My cords may be a size smaller but they've got more give than those things. What do you say we trade? I think we can pin me into your jeans. Okay?"

Foxie gave me a wild look, her eyes so wide I could see white all around the deep blue of the irises. "Just what are you trying to do, Shelley Lucas? You setting me up for another—for another *massacre* out there? Like before?"

Nicole flared up at her. "Shut up and get out of those jeans! Or do you want to wait in here till closing time? And let the waiters have a good laugh while you're running for the door? Listen, you've got ten seconds to make up your mind. Because I think Shelley's insane to bother about somebody like you."

Foxie took a deep shuddering breath, took off

her jeans, and we traded. I'd been right. My cords were a little snug on her, but passable. And Nicole had no problem pinning me into the jeans.

Nicole had clearly worked herself into a fever by that point. She had taken charge, and now she kept a tight grip on the reins. Watching her face, pink with indignation, I wanted to explode with laughter.

"Fine," she said, inspecting us. "Now look. I'll go out first. Foxie, you come after me, right at my heels. Shelley, you stay close to Foxie. We go straight down the center aisle and through the door. We don't stop for anything, even if somebody tries to talk to us on the way. Got it?"

"Gotcha, chief," I said, and smothered a giggle.

"Okay," Foxie muttered.

We marched through Farrell's as if we'd rehearsed the routine. A couple kids called to us, but we stared straight ahead, even ignoring the girls who'd come with Nicole. They followed us outside.

Foxie said in a choked voice, "I'll bring your cords over tomorrow, Shelley. Is that all right?" She took off without waiting for an answer.

"Why that—that ungrateful—that—" Nicole sputtered. "She never even said thanks."

By that time, the whole idiotic incident seemed hysterically funny. I was laughing so hard I couldn't say a word. Jon stood off to one side, smiling a little uncertainly. When Nicole glanced at him, his expression must have set her off. We ended up clutching at each other, rocking with laughter.

"I'll call you," she gasped at last. "Boy, have I missed you, Shell! Look, we've gotta talk. Anybody who'd do what you just did—I'd never find another friend like you. Tomorrow, we'll talk—"

We hugged each other hard. When she turned away, she had tears in her eyes. I couldn't tell whether or not they were tears of laughter. Maybe Nicole wasn't sure, either.

13

The next morning, Emily and I whizzed through the regular Saturday cleaning because Mom said we could decorate the house for Christmas. She had put her foot down about not getting the tree until a week before the big day, but she must have come down with holiday fever early, too. When Emily begged to decorate the rooms, Mom grinned and said, "Sure, go to it. Dad'll get the boxes down for you."

After breakfast we put the album of Christmas music on the stereo, and by ten o'clock Emily and I were digging through the big cartons marked CHRISTMAS in red letters. It's always fun unpacking the things. I forget from year to year exactly what we have, because Mom keeps adding to our assortment of decorations.

We have special candles and a Swiss music box with carvings of the Nativity scene, sets of angels made out of china and wood and brass, and ceramic Santas that dangle from the chandelier over the dining-room table. Red and green mice and bunnies and puppies and kittens look down from their places on top of picture frames and mirrors or peer from the corners of end tables. My favorite Christmas animal is a pixilated rat who hangs by his tail from the handle to the furnace outlet in the living-room ceiling.

Emily and I had just finished putting everything in place and were admiring the effect when the doorbell rang.

"That's Foxie, I bet," I said.

Emily made a face and hurried down the hall to her room.

I found Foxie standing on the top step. She looked at me warily as if she thought I might snatch the cords she held out and slam the door in her face. "Uh—I brought your pants," she said unnecessarily. "I would have been here earlier, but I washed them for you—least I could do—"

"Oh. Well, thanks. Your jeans are in my room. Want to come in?" It startled me when she nodded

172

and followed me through the house. I still had the strong feeling that she'd prefer to swap pants in a hurry and leave. I handed her the jeans. "I hope you're better than I am at putting in zippers—"

"No," she said. "I didn't really come over to get them, just to bring yours back." Her face turned pink. I could see her swallow. "And to tell you—I don't know why you did that for me. Especially after I'd been so mean. But—thanks—"

"It's okay." By that time I felt so uncomfortable I wished she'd go. In fact, I felt sure she'd take off now that she'd managed to blurt out a few gracious words, so I figured it would be safe to ask her to sit down.

She hesitated, glanced around the room, and darned if she didn't sit down on one of the beds. Then, as I settled on the other one, she made a strangled sound and began to cry. It was the craziest thing. One moment, her face twisted. The next, big tears poured down her face.

I leaped up to close the door, though she hadn't made a sound, and got the box of tissues from my bed table. Then I sat beside her, not touching her, just dithering. "There. Oh, Foxie, what's the matter? You aren't crying just because I lent you those pants, are you? Because that sure wasn't much. I'd do that for—" I stopped before I came out with the whole truth, that I would have done it for anyone.

It's a wonder how anybody can talk with a mouth full of feet, but somehow I manage.

"Foxie, please—why are you crying? Did something happen that I don't know about?"

She nodded, gulping convulsively, but it was a while before she could turn off the waterworks. I haven't seen anybody cry that hard since Emily went through a Sarah Heartburn phase in kindergarten. Instant tears were her specialty.

"It's just—" Foxie gave a long hiccuppy sigh. "It's just so lousy—knowing that everybody hates me—"

Naturally, I had to argue with her, but I crossed my fingers to keep my record clean. "You must have a whole bunch of friends. Look at all the guys you've dated. Only they weren't at Farrell's last night when you—"

"When I did my usual number." She blew her nose. "And it backfired. Oh, I'm not bitching about that. I guess—I guess I had it coming. What I didn't expect was—out of everybody there last night— nobody'd lift a finger to help me. You were the only one. Even Nicole wouldn't have bothered. She said so, herself."

She lifted her head to stare at me, blue eyes filling with tears once more. "So how come you went out of your way to— I have to know, Shelley. Why did you do that?"

I chewed my lip. Then I shrugged. "It just seemed as if Jon and I—and those other kids—we'd made our point. Evened the score. Anything beyond that had to be—really rotten."

"You want to know what rotten is?" Foxie said softly. "Rotten's the way other kids treat somebody who weighs a hundred sixty pounds in sixth grade. They come up with names like Lardo and El Slobbo. Rotten is—laughing when a fat kid has a problem fitting in those awful desks. And the cracks they make about food at lunchtime—"

I said, puzzled, "But you—you aren't fat."

"In sixth grade I was. Even my mom got disgusted after a while. I wouldn't stay on a diet, so she sent me to a fat farm. It's down by San Diego, way back in the mountains. Three months of exercise, terrible food, and a bunch of blubbery kids, all of them just as miserable as I was. I took off almost fifty pounds before I came back to start junior high."

"Fifty pounds! Wow!"

She went on as if she hadn't heard me. I doubt if she did. She sat staring off in space as if she were talking to herself, trying to figure something out.

"Those kids at the farm—you'd think we'd have tried to help each other. All of us in the same boat, stuck off in the boonies with sadistic people driving us every minute of the day. Running, swimming, tennis, sweating off the flab. So hungry we could die, and nothing but dumb vegetables and salads and—"

She looked at me and made a sharp gesture. "Listen, we all hated ourselves so much it seemed like we hated everybody. Even each other. Those fat kids were so mean, they made the kids back home look like—like plaster saints. I used to cry myself to sleep every night till I got tough enough to fight back.

"My folks moved across town that summer, so I started school with a different group of kids. There I was, down to the right weight, with a lot of terrific new clothes. People seemed to be impressed, you know? Especially the guys."

She took a deep breath. "But something had happened to me. In grammar school, when someone got really nasty, I just used to *think* of things to say. At the farm, I learned to say them, every ugly thing that came into my head. When I came back home, I—I kept on saying them, even when there wasn't a reason anymore to rip people." She ended harshly, "I'm still doing it, I guess. I don't seem to know how to stop."

I leaned back and stared at her until she finally glanced at me. "What's the matter? Don't you believe me?"

"Sure. It's just that—I never realized before how much we have in common."

Foxie gave a short laugh, but it sounded strained. "Yeah, sure. We're a *lot* alike. Except that everybody thinks you're fantastic. Little and cute and funny and—"

"That's the word, all right. Funny. Foxie, you slammed me about that yourself! About me being a clown all the time. Didn't you know it was an act? I couldn't believe anybody would like me unless I came on strong every single minute. Always on, knocking myself out. And hating it. Hating myself more and more, just like you did."

"You?" Her eyes were wide. "Well, yeah, come to think of it, you aren't on that trip anymore. But I thought it was only around me, because I turned you off. And you're so crazy about Jon—"

I told her what he'd said about my funny-lady role and how that helped me get my act together. Strange. It seemed that I became aware of a lot of things even as I put them into words.

"I figure if my family likes me—the way I really am—and Megan and Nicole do, too—and Jon, of course—well, I must be doing okay. Besides, if I keep on pretending to be somebody I'm not, how am I going to know who truly cares about *me*? The person I really am."

Foxie nodded. "I don't know why I'm sitting here bending your ear," she said a little sheepishly. "I just had to find out why you got me off the hook last night. And you never even called me Gwendolyn. But why should I lay all this stuff on you, hoping you'd help—after what you've already done—"

"Did any of this help? Do you feel better now?"

She sighed. "Sure. Now if I could believe that I could change, too, like you did—only I've got a thousand miles more to go—"

"Of course you can change," I said from my vast wisdom.

"How?"

Before I could stop myself, I burst out with "Start by biting your tongue a lot," and then wished I'd taken my own advice.

But Foxie just laughed a little shakily. "I'll never have the kind of friends you do, even if I try to be nice."

"Give it time. Come back to the clown class," I suggested. "We're going out to Sunnyside tomorrow. Why don't you come, too?"

She finally said she would. Then she picked up her jeans and left so quickly I had a hunch she was on the verge of tears again. As I closed the front door, I heard the phone ring.

Mom called to me from the kitchen. "It's Nicole,"

she said happily. "Why don't you ask her for lunch?"

But Nicole said she'd already eaten. "Megan's here, and we're both dying to know if Foxie ever showed up and—can you come over?"

"I'll grab a sandwich first. I'm running a little late, because—matter of fact, I've been talking to Foxie. Declared a truce, you might say."

"Bet she buried the hatchet right between your eyes." Her voice was wry. "Okay, eat fast. We want to hear every word you said."

An hour later, after I'd replayed that extraordinary conversation, Nicole pretended to fall back on her bed in total shock.

Megan clucked sympathetically. She was sitting on the rug with Nicole's puppy curled in her lap. "It explains a lot," she said. "Kids can be awfully mean, especially when somebody looks different. A really fat girl—in sixth grade—I can imagine how they treated her. And then that terrible fat farm. It isn't any wonder she ended up with a curdled personality."

I nodded. "Anyway, she promised to show up tomorrow. And I'm for—well, giving her another chance. Maybe she'll shape up. I mean, now that she knows where she went off the track—"

Nicole said lightly, "Maybe there's a human being buried inside that gorgeous bod. Way *way* inside." She sat up in time to catch Megan's thoughtful glance.

179

"Okay, okay. Only reason I got mad at her in the first place was because of the way she treated Shell."

I smiled at her, feeling great because we were back together again, like always.

"I wrote a letter to Byron, Shell," she said then, awkwardly. "Too chicken to call him. But I did write and tell him I'm sorry. Would you give him the letter tonight? You think—you think there's any chance he'll forgive me?"

"Yes and yes."

Just as I thought about the one thing still unresolved that would make everything pink and perfect, Nicole brought that up, too.

"I'm going out to Sunnyside tomorrow." She cleared her throat.

"Hey, that—that's terrific."

"I'm not making any excuses. I know I acted like a real nerd. But—maybe I'm like Foxie, too. I want people to know *why* I did all those dumb things. Because I was scared, that's why. Panicky. Granny Gus loves me better than anybody in the whole world. I—I still can't bear to think about her—taking the first step—away—"

When she hesitated, I had to swallow a lump in my throat. I guess that's what she was doing, too.

"So, anyway"—she reeled in a long breath—"I finally realized—when you told me off, Shell, that day at the hospital—Granny's always been there for me when I needed her. Now it's my turn to help her. I was furious at you that day, but—you were right."

She straightened, her eyes shiny with tears. "Let's talk about something else quick, or I'll cry. Say something funny, Shell. Please."

I discovered I couldn't think of one tired feeble line, not if my life depended on it. Megan sat biting her lip, her eyes imploring me to come to the rescue.

As it turned out, Nicole's fat, funny puppy saved the day. He rolled onto his back, opened his mouth in an enormous yawn, and squealed, a sound startlingly close to laughter.

14

The Sunnyside trip turned out a lot better than I'd dared to hope. Granny Gus and Tillie were there, sitting in the background, applauding enthusiastically. All the old people gathered in the colorfully decorated recreation room seemed to enjoy the clowns that day.

I kept an eye on Nicole, but she came through like a champ. Of course it would have been impossible to feel much tension, surrounded by a laughing crowd like that one. Even Foxie looked as if she were having a wonderful time.

After we did our skits, we walked around to talk to the people. I noticed right away how their faces lit up, how they'd reach out to touch us. Obviously, they were lonesome, and it made me sad to realize they didn't have enough visitors. But it was more than that.

One tiny wrinkled lady not much bigger than Megan smiled up at me and held my hand between hers. "Oh, honey, it's been so long since I've seen somebody young," she said. "You're a breath of fresh air, like spring coming early. The sight of you young folks and the sound of your voices—it makes me remember when I was your age—so many happy things—"

I didn't realize that anyone else in our group felt as I did until a week later. Nicole, Megan, and I compared notes when we got together to compose the final résumés for our 4-H notebooks. We all had practically identical reactions to the class as far as the learning stages were concerned. But in the last section, we each described ways we had grown through the clowning experience.

Nicole told about the trip to Sunnyside that had been so difficult for her. "Some of the old people were like children. We had to approach them slowly so we wouldn't frighten them. But when they understood that we were clowns, that we'd come to visit and have fun with them, they laughed and had a great time. I came home feeling good, really glad that I went. I want to make sure I don't forget these experiences. So I've given my puppy my clown name—Bubble Bum."

Megan's paper revealed her delight in finding clowning "something I'm good at!" She went on and on about the kids, naturally, and how neat it was to make them laugh. "Most of all," she wrote, "it was wonderful to discover that it's really true—a person's looks aren't important. It's the inside of a person that counts in clowning, because nobody can tell what a clown really looks like. That's how I found out something else that's good to know. The people I truly love—and my very closest friends—don't care about looks."

Hurray for Mark, I thought. Megan had to wait until she was fifteen to realize that people love her for the person she is inside. But better late than never.

I decided to write about the day we went to the children's ward and I met Sam. I ended by telling how she felt about the clowns. I hope that's the kind of thing Mrs. De Witt wants for this page in my notebook. Anyway, it was the most fantastic highlight for me.

I'll never forget that little kid, lonesome and hurting a lot, and how she said I made her forget the pain for a while, losing it in laughter. I didn't add Sam's final comment, how she loved Acey Deucey but she liked Shelley even better. That's too personal. But I'll sure remember what she said if I ever get confused again.

It seems crazy that I had to become another person to find out who I really want to be. Acey Deucey is fun, but only on a part-time basis, only when I choose to be a clown. From now on, I'll concentrate on being Shelley Elizabeth Lucas. With all my potential . . .